PUFFIN BO

Editor: Kaye

THE PECULIAR TRIUMPH OF PROFESSOR BRANESTAWM

Poor Professor Branestawm, even his best inventions seem to lead to trouble, as he found with his new getting-you-dressed machine, his invaluable translating machine for holidays abroad, and his extremely useful device for bringing up babies' wind, not to mention his Stratospheric Limousine and his greatest triumph of all, his neat solution to Pagwell's parking problems.

The eccentric old professor first appeared in the 1930s, but genius often burns brighter with age, and he is certainly just as ingenious and gets into as many unfortunate predicaments in this collection of stories as he does in the many other volumes available in Puffins.

Norman Hunter can also write about conjuring tricks which really do work, and if you don't believe it you should take a look at *The Puffin Book of Magic*.

For everyone over eight who enjoys a good laugh, especially boys.

The Peculiar Triumph of
Professor Branestawm

NORMAN HUNTER

with illustrations by George Adamson

PUFFIN BOOKS
in association with The Bodley Head

Puffin Books, Penguin Books Ltd, Harmondsworth, Middlesex, England
Penguin Books, 625 Madison Avenue, New York, New York 10022, U.S.A.
Penguin Books Australia Ltd, Ringwood, Victoria, Australia
Penguin Books Canada Ltd, 2801 John Street, Markham, Ontario, Canada L3R 1B4
Penguin Books (N.Z.) Ltd, 182–190 Wairau Road, Auckland 10, New Zealand

—

First published by The Bodley Head 1970
Published in Puffin Books 1972
Reprinted in 1973, 1974, 1975, 1977, 1980
Professor Branestawm's Christmas Tree
published in *Puffin Post* 1969
Peril at Pagwell College published by Penguin Books
in *The Friday Miracle and Other Stories*, 1969

—

Copyright © Norman Hunter, 1970
Illustrations copyright © The Bodley Head, 1970

—

Set, printed and bound in Great Britain by
Cox & Wyman Ltd, Reading
Set in Monotype Baskerville

To Sir Allen Lane
who was a kind of Fairy Godfather to the
Professor because he handled the production
of the very first Branestawm book.

Contents

Acknowledgement

In *The Unexpected Tale of Professor Flittersnoop* the idea for the machine came from Kay Trenholme and Gregory Mason who won first prize between them in a Branestawm invention competition run by Puffin Books, and from Maxim Everest-Phillips, Matthew Wiggans, Pauline Hart and Jessica Norrie, who sent in similar ideas.

Branestawm's Broadcasting Clarifier

THE Mayor of Pagwell was reclining municipally in his sitting-room listening to a brass band concert, when suddenly the music stopped, and, instead, out of his radio came instructions on how to make a suet pudding.

Dr Mumpzanmeazle was listening hurriedly to a talk on spots while he had his dinner, accompanied by four patients who were waiting to have their hearts listened to. All at once, the spots talk changed to some very spotted music full of hotcha cha chas and pom pa tiddley om pa's.

The Vicar of Pagwell was enjoying an organ recital given by some organ that didn't seem to need any money spent on it, which was quite a change, when the organ unexpectedly gave place to a lot of last year's jokes told very rapidly by someone who didn't seem to see them.

Monsieur Bonmonjay, the Manager of Pagwell Central Hotel, was listening to some highly prancy music to which his hotel guests were politely dancing. Then zonk! The prancy music was swamped by excerpts from the Life of Mary Queen of Scots followed by a strong letter to the Gas Company about quantities of new pence.

An exciting running commentary on international Rugby, which the Pagwell College Games Master was enjoying, changed into a cradle song from three shrill sopranos, and Colonel Dedshott of the Catapult Cavaliers, listening fiercely to the weather report heard it turn first into a most unmili-

tary song about the Navy and then into a learned discourse
on the habits of field mice.

'Disgraceful, by Jove,' the Colonel roared, twiddling
knobs, which made no difference. 'Don't know what the
programmes are coming to, my word. What do we pay
goodness knows how much a year tax for?'

'The privilege of remaining away from work when one is
unwell,' said the radio, starting on a talk about insurances.

'Confound it, sir, where is the weather?' growled the
Colonel, turning everything round as far as it would go.

'Stormy weather,' sang the radio, changing its mind
again.

'Pah!' snorted the Colonel, turning it off altogether.

'Whereas the difference between points "A" and "B" is
exactly half the – um – ah – distance between points – er –
"C" and – ah – "D",' went on the radio, taking no notice
and going all geometric.

'Branestawm!' cried the Colonel, recognizing the voice.

'Four shirts, six collars, one pillow slip,' continued the
radio.

It was certainly the voice of Professor Branestawm. But
where was it coming from, how was it coming through a
turned-off radio and why was it talking about laundry and
other nonsense?

'Boil briskly for three minutes and allow to – ah – cool,'
went on the voice.

Colonel Dedshott fired off orders at his Catapult Cavalier
Butlers, and left the house on his horse with the Professor's
voice telling him where to go for his summer holiday.

'My word! By Jove! Confound it, sir, what!' gasped the
Colonel as he looked up at the Professor's windows.

Sparks a foot long were dancing round the window frames.
Sizzlings and cracklings were taking place. The entire house

seemed to be continually being struck by lightning in a small way.

Mrs Flittersnoop, the Professor's housekeeper, was on her way back from staying with her sister Aggie in Lower Pagwell during the Professor's last busting up invention. She arrived just in time to let the Colonel in with her. He clattered upstairs and found the Professor surrounded by unreasonable machinery and super-charged science. Crackle, crackle, pop, bang, whiz, wow-w-w-w-w. Sparks shot about. Retorts and reports were everywhere. The Professor, wearing his five pairs of spectacles and three pairs of headphones, had a microphone which looked like a hat box on legs, in front of him. He was frantically reading out snatches from books,

bits from old letters and circulars, and playing small helpings of gramophone records while he scribbled notes on the backs of the letters he was reading from. Now and again he read out his own notes by mistake which didn't seem to matter much, except that they gave rise to a lot more notes.

'I – ah – what, hum, by Jove, yes!' spluttered the Colonel, jingling his medals.

But the Professor was so absolutely neck-tie and collar-stud deep in his experiments that the Colonel had to drop three flatulents hums over the ranks before he could attract his attention.

'Ah, Dedshott, there you are,' said the Professor, pulling ear-phones and spectacles off himself like plums off a tree. 'You are just in time, Dedshott, to see something of the first experiments I am making with an entirely new discovery.'

'Ha!' said the Colonel, sitting heavily on a chair but getting up again at once as the chair had a pointed something on it.

'B.B.C.', said the Professor pressing a switch and letting half a yard of green flame out of a jar.

'By Jove!' cried the Colonel.

'Branestawm's Broadcasting Clarifier,' explained the Professor, permitting purple and green sparks of different lengths to mix together, when they went up in black steam and high speed howlings. 'As you know, Dedshott, the reception of broadcast programmes is sometimes interfered with by the operation of electric trains, refrigerators and other domestic machinery. I have abolished this interference by the simple process, Dedshott, of planning my broadcasting on the same lines as the interference which previously interfered with it. You understand. If trains interfere with radio, then radio should be designed on the train lines so – er – to speak, Dedshott. The design of the interference then be-

comes the design of the broadcasting, and the more it inter-
feres the better.'

'Marvellous!' said the Colonel.

Just then, Mrs Flittersnoop came in to say some gentlemen
had called from the Pagwell Broadcasting Company.

'Ah yes, – er – show them in, Mrs Flittersnoop, by all
means,' said the Professor.

Mrs Flittersnoop showed them in by all the means she
could think of, which consisted of opening the door and
letting them walk in.

'Everything is ready for the – ah – demonstration of my
non-interference broadcasting system,' said the Professor,
sorting out flashes of lightning into different lengths.

'It must stop at once!' said one of the broadcasting gentlemen.

'This switch,' said the Professor, 'controls the atmospheric
out-put transformer.'

'Turn it off!' commanded another broadcasting gentleman.

'By making adjustments on this dial it becomes possible to
control the tone, volume and balance,' went on the Professor.

Two of the broadcasting gentlemen sat on the apparatus,
which instantly went up in coloured sparks and assorted
shrieks.

'By Jove!' gasped the Colonel.

'Tut, tut,' said the Professor, peering severely over and
under pairs of spectacles at the broadcasting gentlemen.

'I wish, gentlemen, that you would be – ah – good enough
not to interfere with the apparatus. It is extremely delicate.'

Another broadcasting gentleman began bashing about the
works with a hammer.

'How dare you?' spluttered the Professor. 'You will ruin
the work of a lifetime. Good gracious! I – ah – er – stop!'

Crash, wallop, bang! Broadcasting gentlemen set about the Professor's invention with flat irons, hockey sticks and pokers.

'By Jove, we can't have this, you know. Confound it, sir. Play the game, what!' roared Colonel Dedshott. The Colonel always reckoned it was his job to smash the Professor's inventions when they got out of hand, but this one didn't seem to be giving any trouble at all. Most unfair. Considerably unsporting. Zang, biff, whiz! The sparks grew longer and longer. Puffs of smoke began to go up. Soon the Professor's apparatus was in ruins, and the Professor was dancing with rage.

'I – I – I – have the goodness to fetch the police, Dedshott,' spluttered the Professor. 'Disgraceful! I invite you gentlemen here to a demonstration of the greatest radio invention of our time, and this is how you – um – ah – behave.'

'We didn't get your invitation, Professor,' said the broadcasting gentlemen soothingly. 'We came of our own accord. Your invention has been causing considerable annoyance to listeners.'

'I have removed interference from broadcasting,' cried the Professor.

'You have made yourself a most scientific nuisance with probably the best intentions,' explained the broadcasting gentlemen. 'Nobody could listen to anything but you. But everything will be all right now, I am sure. Good day to you, Professor.' And they filed politely out and went back to the Pagwell Broadcasting Company to arrange more and longer helpings of chamber music.

'Well, that seems to be rather that, what!' said the Colonel.

But if the broadcasting gentlemen thought they had settled things, they were mistaken. The following morning, Mrs Flittersnoop was cooking sausages for breakfast, when they shouted at her from the frying-pan.

The Mayor of Pagwell was about to lay a foundation stone when it burst into a song about roses and love.

The Vicar's second best hat spoke off a sermon all by itself, which might have saved him the trouble of writing one, only it was hanging on the back of the scullery door and he didn't hear it. The scullery door replied with careful instructions on what to do for an escape of gas.

Colonel Dedshott's sideboard issued a warning against leaving off one's woollen underwear too soon, and the tradesmen's entrance at Pagwell Hotel discussed smoke abatement at great length with the nearest lamp post; while the Pagwell Games Master received the year-before-last's cricket scores combined with the price of Brussels sprouts from a photograph of his cousin Nancy.

'Dear me, this is most extraordinary,' muttered the Professor interrupting a spot of part singing by his five pairs of spectacles, 'but most instructive. I must write a paper on it though I cannot account for it.'

'Will you have a chop for dinner, sir?' asked Mrs Flittersnoop.

'Chop the wood into short sticks and tie into bundles,' replied the mantelpiece.

'Begging your pardon, sir?' said Mrs Flittersnoop.

'Er, yes, yes, of course,' said the Professor.

The curtains broke into a stirring military march just in time to herald the entrance of Colonel Dedshott, whose medals were arguing about the price of coke.

'Good morning, sir,' said Mrs Flittersnoop.

'Weather will be milder throughout the day. Mix carefully with a wooden spoon and if the matter is not attended to without delay, we shall take steps to lend me your ears. I come to bury Caesar, not to pom tiddley om pom tanta ra ra pom,' answered the coalscuttle.

'By Jove!' cried the Colonel. 'Built your invention again Branestawm? You'll have the Pagwell Broadcasting Company round, you know. Risky business, what!'

'Dedshott?' said the Professor suddenly jumping up and beginning to walk rapidly up and down while the furniture played selections from famous operas. 'I believe you may possibly be right. Be good enough to come with me, Dedshott. This matter must be – er – sifted to the – um – ah – bottom.'

The Professor shot hurriedly out of the house followed by the Colonel, who understood nothing as usual, but intended to be there when it happened.

Professor Branestawm walked very determinedly into the high class premises of the Pagwell Broadcasting Company. Reception gentlemen swept forward to meet him with forms to be filled up. He ploughed through them. Two commissionaire gentlemen came out of cubby holes to stop him. But they caught sight of Colonel Dedshott, and seeing he had more medals than they had, they stopped to salute before throwing him out. By the time they came unsaluted, the Colonel was clattering up the stairs behind the Professor who was muttering scientific conversation to himself.

Along corridors they charged. Past doors, from behind which came the sound of typewriters and tea. Past notices which said 'Private' and 'Keep Out' and 'Do not Enter', and 'Turn back at Once'. Ladies of all ages shot past them carrying baskets of broadcastery business. Then the Professor pushed open a door marked 'Broadcasting Apparatus, Deadly Private', and they arrived in a room full of machinery.

'Kindly fasten the door, Dedshott,' said the Professor arranging his spectacles and taking two folding hammers from his pocket.

'What's the idea, Branestawm?' asked the Colonel.

'It takes the form of retributionary action, Dedshott,' said the Professor. 'It is only logical that as officials have destroyed the apparatus with which I was apparently causing, quite innocently, a certain amount of disturbance among listeners, I should in turn – ah – dismantle the apparatus with which seemingly the Pagwell Broadcasting Company are causing even more annoyance.' He brought down his hammer on the machinery, which gave him a puff of smoke for his trouble.

'This is against the law, you know,' protested the Colonel, taking the other hammer and sloshing away with sparks going up in strings all over the place.

In the meantime, the broadcasting gentlemen had gone to call on Professor Branestawm again. They burst into the Professor's Broadcasting Room with hammers of their own. But they fell back in dismay. There was no apparatus there.

Strange. Professor Branestawm wasn't causing the unwanted broadcasts. Neither was Pagwell Broadcasting Company, although Professor Branestawm thought they were.

Professor Branestawm and Colonel Dedshott were hard at it, full steam up. Smash, bang, wallop, crack. Bits of apparatus flew about. Smoke and sparks. 'By Jove, sir!' Crash! 'This is – um – ah – only just I think.' Sizz, pouff, wowo! 'By gad!' Jangle, jingle.

Twice the Professor hit the Colonel on the medals by mistake. Once the Colonel nearly hit the apparatus with the Professor.

Then the door flew open and broadcasting people flew in upon them.

'Do your worst, by Jove!' said the Colonel throwing out his chest so violently that six medals shot off and landed in a cup of tea someone had with him.

Then Mrs Flittersnoop arrived with the police, most of

whom were friends of hers or related in complicated ways to sister Aggie.

Purple pandemonium raged. In the middle of it the Professor was hit with a penetrating idea. He saw what was the matter. Perhaps too late, but still, he saw, which was something. But he couldn't make himself heard. Then a heavy clock struck going-home time. Instantly nearly all the broadcasting people disappeared in the direction of hats and coats, and the Professor and the Colonel were left with two very involved broadcasting gentlemen in fancy waistcoats.

'The saturation of non-screened bodies with radio waves,' cried the Professor, waving spectacles.

'What say?' asked the broadcasting gentlemen.

'Don't you see?' cried the Professor. 'My broadcasting apparatus was intensely powerful. It had to be in order to overcome interference. Continual broadcasting from it saturated the surrounding buildings and objects with radio emanations.'

'By Jove, wonderful!' said the Colonel, reckoning he must stick up for the Professor whatever it was all about.

'Now that the broadcasting from my apparatus has been terminated,' went on the Professor, 'the buildings and other objects for a considerable radius of my – ah – station, being saturated with the broadcast waves, will continue to – ah – re-radiate them until the force is spent.'

'Like luminous paint sort of soaks up light and gives it out again,' said one of the broadcasting gentlemen.

'Aye,' said the other one.

Things were explained. It took days for the unofficial broadcastings, that Professor Branestawm had been letting off, to die away and so assorted surprise items kept cropping up now and again.

'But,' said the Professor, looking round at the smashed machinery, 'I fear we have done irreparable damage to your broadcasting apparatus. How about the Pagwell programmes?'

'Oh, that's all right, Professor,' said the gentlemen, patting their fancy waistcoats. 'This is a special room we keep full of discarded apparatus so that if anyone gets really cross with us because we don't broadcast the sort of things he likes, and comes round all truculent, we just let him loose in here, and after an hour or two he goes away happy, thinking he has smashed the works.'

'Um – ah,' said the Professor. That was an idea he hadn't thought of. He went slowly home working out plans for a special kind of dummy invention of his own that could be left about for smashing purposes to save his real ones, in case of emergency. There was one thing about it. Such an invention wouldn't have to work, and couldn't very well go wrong.

2

The Professor Goes All Horticultural

To look at Professor Branestawm as he walked into the front garden of his friend, Colonel Dedshott, anyone might have been excused for thinking it was a flag day. He looked, in fact, as if it was every flag day ever thought of, all occurring at once. Not that he wore any flags; he wore a flower, which is what one often gets made to wear on a flag day. But what a flower was the Professor's!

To begin with it was square. To go on with, it was a foot across. To go further, each petal was a different colour. To go a lot too far, the centre was like an exceedingly twiddly door knob; and to finish most sensationally up with, the flower had a perfume; no, not a perfume, a smell rather, or perhaps a hum, like fifteen wet washing days flavoured with paregoric and a touch of gas escape.

'Branestawm's Obnoxious Grandiflora, Dedshott,' said the Professor. 'A little – er – invention of my own.'

'Confound it, Branestawm, you can't *invent* flowers!' exclaimed the Colonel. 'The things just grow, by Jove!'

'I have brought science to the aid of nature, Dedshott,' replied the Professor. 'By means of certain – ah – special basic and progressive fertilizers allied to complex systems of grafting,' the Professor waved his hands and pairs of spectacles flew about, 'I am able to produce a considerable number and variety of flowers, totally unlike the ordinary blossoms with which we have hitherto been – ah – acquainted. The one you see before you is a sample.'

'Marvellous, by Jove, what!' grunted the Colonel. Just then Mrs Flittersnoop, the Professor's housekeeper, arrived with an urgent message. People were calling on the Professor. Did he wish to see them or should she say he was out, which he certainly was?

At Professor Branestawm's house, half the Professor's inventory had been turned into a highly drastic conservatory occupied by outrageous plants. It was also occupied to some extent by a Pagwell Councillor who kept a flower shop in the day-time, and Dr Mumpzanmeazle, who grew flowers for a hobby and found it a nice change to look at something that didn't have to put its tongue out immediately.

'We have called on behalf of the Great and Little Pagwell Horticultural Friendly Society,' began the Councillor.

'Which meets twice a month in my dining room,' added the Doctor.

'To ask you to exhibit your inventions at a flower show,' went on the Councillor.

'As the time does not interfere with my dinner,' put in the Doctor.

'I think I could persuade the Countess of Pagwell to open it,' continued the Councillor.

'With the furniture pushed back against the wall,' added the Doctor, still talking about his dining room.

While Colonel Dedshott was trying to sort out this conversation into two complete sets, the Professor had gone off into flower demonstrations among his inventions.

'Here we have the Climbing Scrambularis or Staircase Rose,' he said, pointing to a long skinny plant that went up the wall in jerks and finished at the top in one frightful flower, blue and orange stripes with black tassels hanging from it.

'Bit untidy, what?' grunted the Colonel, who didn't agree

much with ramblers, but preferred hollyhocks as they looked more military.

'This is the – um – ah – Grandifloris Grandiflora Grandiflorum,' went on the Professor, pointing to a bicycle-shaped flower.

'Very fine,' said the Pagwell Councillor. He stroked the flower and it rang a bell at him.

'The Hybrid Holdoff or Unpickable Posy. A little idea of mine for front gardens and public parks,' explained the Professor. 'It makes makes forbidding the public to pluck flowers quite ah – unnecessary. Be good enough to try to pick one, Doctor.'

The Doctor tried. Good gracious! The flower dodged him. He tried again. The blossom swung round and tapped him playfully on the nose. Colonel Dedshott had a go, but the flower bobbed round and knocked his hat off.

'As you were, by Jove!' grunted the Colonel, and while he was still trying to pick the unpickable posy, the Professor showed the others the rest of the plants.

There was the Early Closing Opplebopple which blossomed on Wednesday afternoons and smelt of peppermint.

There was the Dry Growing Brollybloom, a sort of cactus that not only didn't need any watering but which, if you did water it, instantly came out in little green umbrellas all over itself.

There was also a very modern plant which had chromium-plated flowers and glass leaves; another whose flowers grew straight out of the earth without any stalks or leaves and fell to bits as soon as they came up, and an excessively fat little specimen with revolving blossoms.

Finally there was a quite ordinary-looking rose that smelt like a carnation and had rhubarb-shaped leaves, and a couple of very affectionate plants that would grow tied together and come out in each other's flowers by mistake.

'All this is very interesting, Professor Branestawm,' said the Pagwell Councillor. 'If I might suggest it, they would cause quite a stir at our flower show.'

'Yes, of course,' said Professor Branestawm. Anybody might suggest that his inventions would cause a stir if exhibited anywhere, and he would not contradict them.

The Pagwell Flower Show and Branestawm Exhibition was a great success. In fact, it was more like a circus and fun fair than a flower show. The Professor's inventions made such good side shows that quite a number of them were divided off, and special admissions were charged. Prizes were offered to anyone who could pick the unpickable posy. And seeing that nobody could pick it, the prizes were exceedingly handsome.

'I think, Dedshott,' said the Professor over a cup of tea in the refreshment buffet, 'that I have at last invented an – um – ah – invention which is incapable of going wrong or of causing any inconvenience.'

'Bravo!' grunted the Colonel, putting out his hand for a cake, but finding the Professor had already put them all in his pocket.

'Perfectly too marvellous, my dear Professor,' said the Countess of Pagwell, 'these plants of yours. I really must take home that positively sweet little plant that puts its umbrellas up at you. Oh, and the one that scrambles about; I simply must have that. It would look too perfectly fitting in my pink and orange boudoir.'

'Quite agree with you, my dear Countess,' said the Honourable Horace Hownow, who always went about with her when she opened places, carrying his top hat and making the affair look terribly important. 'I shall buy the one with the revolving blossoms. Nobody will believe it. What great fun!'

Plant buying soon became earnest. The Mayor of Pagwell took home the Piano Peony and stood it on his grand piano.

Colonel Dedshott, who would rather have left the Professor's plants severely alone, felt he must back up his friend. So he marched off with the Early Closing Opplebopple, even though he disliked peppermint.

Dr Mumpzanmeazle had the twin plants tied together, and the Vicar of Pagwell chose the unpickable posy, while the plant with the bicycle-shaped flowers was carried, ringing furiously, to the fire station, where it probably felt quite at home.

'Excellent!' said the Professor. 'This flower-growing business is most satisfactory. I wonder I did not think of it before. No machinery to get out of order. Nothing to cause trouble. The flowers are, I fear, of no practical value, but they are most interesting.'

Three days later the insects appeared.

The Countess of Pagwell was in the middle of an exceedingly high class and expensive tea party when someone poured tea leaves into the Dry Growing Brollybloom to see its umbrellas go up. They went up all right. Oh, yes. And out from under them came spiders. In bowler hats! Whackers! Most threatening.

'Help!' shrieked the Countess, ringing for more maids than she had, and fainting among the cushions whose colour went best with her frock.

But that wasn't all. Oh dear no! There were greenfly on the staircase rose. But the greenfly were blue and yellow. They came into the boudoir in rows and lapped up all the milk.

The Honourable Horace burst in to say that whirling grasshoppers and caterpillars on roller skates were coming out of the plant with revolving blossoms.

'Fetch the Police! Call the Fire Brigade!' squealed the Countess, coming unfainted and drinking someone else's tea.

Alas, the fire station was too busy trying to get rid of exceedingly rapid earwigs with pumped up legs and leather ears that were rushing out of the bicycle plant. And the police had already been called to the Vicar's where the unpickable posy had been picked by determined ants of various colours, three inches long and with too many eyes.

'Dear me!' murmured the Professor when he heard. 'Insects! Yes, yes, of course. Er – ah – um – I fear I had overlooked the question of possibly appropriate insects.'

He opened the door of the conservatory, where he kept the carnation-smelling rhubarb-leaved rose.

Good gracious! The place was full of custard-coloured spiders with pink buttonholes.

'Insecticide!' said the Professor firmly.

He seized a syringe of his own invention, filled with insect-killing stuff of his own mixing.

'Pwouff! Squish!' Clouds of deadly spray shot out towards the spiders. They sat up and begged for more.

'Um!' murmured the Professor. 'More drastic measures appear to be necessary.'

He tried all the drastic measures he and Mrs Flittersnoop could think of, which included treacle spread on newspaper, paraffin and cold coffee and liquorice allsorts minced up small with iron filings and gunpowder. But the only drastic measure that seemed to have any effect was hitting the spiders individually and firmly with a wooden mallet, and this took too long because they were good at dodging.

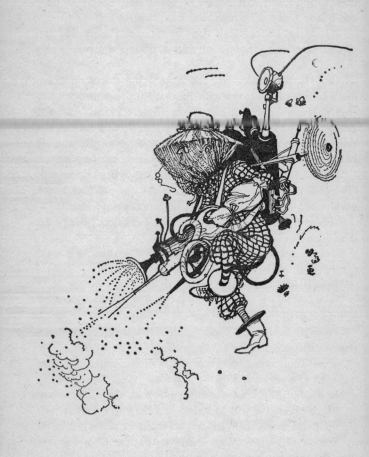

Meantime Dr Mumpzanmeazle returned from visiting spotty patients to find his twin plants had not only come out in each other's blossoms but they were also sharing three kinds of spotty beetles in spectacles. He hurriedly turned on some gassy stuff he kept for operations which put the beetles to sleep. But they snored so loudly that he was thankful when they woke up again.

Within a week the countryside from Great Pagwell to Little Pagwell and from Pagwell Docks to Upper-down-by Dale Pagwell was over-run with ninety-five different kinds of unlikely insects.

They got into the gas pipes and came out fried whenever the gas was lit. They invaded the railways, travelling under the seats, putting their heads out of the windows, and alighting while the trains were in motion, in defiance of all the most deadly rules. They got into the public libraries and played havoc with the punctuation. They could be seen at more cinemas than Tom and Jerry.

'Something must be done about this!' cried the Mayor at a drastically extraordinary meeting of the Pagwell Council.

'Put another tuppence on the rates,' said a Councillor who lived on a boat and didn't have to pay rates.

'Bigger drains will be necessary,' said the Draining Councillor seeing his chance to have exciting things done, with all the roads in Pagwell up at once.

'The Bye-laws must be revised,' declared the Town Clerk, working out fifteen Don'ts and twenty-seven Prohibiteds.

Then the Council went away to lunch, but found insects had got there first and had eaten everything but the bones, of which there were all too few, as lunch was to have been corned beef, cabbage and pickled onions.

'Disgraceful! Something has got to be done!' cried all the Councillors at once, except the last year's Mayor, who kept a grocer's shop and had brought himself biscuits in an insect-proof tin.

Professor Branestawm invented five different kinds of insect-exterminating machinery, three of which didn't work, one nearly exterminated Pagwell Council, and one blew up after dealing with three helpings of pink bluebottles.

Professor Branestawm compounded assorted kinds of insect powder, some of which was in sticks, some in liquid form, some in capsules and none of it in powder. The insects ignored it, and it simply made the place look untidy.

Professor Branestawm invented three special kinds of unpleasant gas. The first two kinds were found to do very well for cooking by, which caused trouble at the Gas Company; while a third sort caused rhubarb to grow circular instead of long shaped, but was otherwise useless.

'Mix 'em all together!' snapped Colonel Dedshott.

'Er – ah – um – I fear the result may be rather dangerous,' said the Professor, mixing them.

The result was to kill off all the Professor's queer plants without harming a single crazy insect.

'It's no use,' said the Mayor. 'Pagwell is insect ridden. We shall have to leave the towns and villages and live somewhere else.' He began to draft drastic notices for posting outside the Town Hall; got as far as 'Whereas' and found three kinds of knitted caterpillars on stilts had drunk all the ink.

Professor Branestawm went for a ride on a bus to think out ideas.

The situation was terrible.

Thank goodness it didn't last long. Soon after the Professor's queer plants had been killed off the crazy insects began to disappear. Gradually they sizzled up and went to powder. Perhaps because they were homesick, or perhaps because not. In less than ten days not a bowler-hatted spider nor a roller-skating beetle was to be seen. And more than that, the crazy insects had so discouraged the ordinary sorts that Pagwell's crop of flowers and fruit was the finest ever known.

Professor Branestawm invented an absolutely certain powder for exterminating the queer insects the day after the last one had gone. But Mrs Flittersnoop was able to use it, mixed with a little vanilla essence and turpentine, for cleaning finger marks off fruit.

3

Penny-in-the-Slot Poetry

THERE seemed to be something different about Great Pagwell. There was a strange feeling about the place. A sort of
unusual calmness. A complete absence of the sensation
usually noticeable in Pagwell that something was about to
take place, nobody knew what but probably something
drastic.

In fact, Professor Branestawm was away.

He was on the pier at Paddledown Bay with Colonel
Dedshott, letting himself loose among the penny-in-the-slot
machines.

'Um – er – ah – most instructive,' said the Professor. He
put a coin into a machine shaped like a very large home-made
chicken which instantly made a noise like three steam
mangles driven by radio and presented him with a blue tin
egg containing three teeny sweets.

'Rather, by Jove, what!' grunted the Colonel, helping
to eat the sweets.

'I am working out a system by means of which the principle
of the slot machine may be adapted to more instructive
ends, Dedshott,' went on the Professor, talking as if he had
been working it out for years when actually he had only that
second thought about it.

On the way back from the pier he happened to find a
book of poetry in a second hand shop where he was buying
three parts of a collapsed typewriter and a set of retired fire
irons for inventing purposes.

The result, when the Professor returned to Pagwell, was Branestawm's penny-in-the-slot poetry machine.

'I venture to think, Dedshott,' said the Professor, having hauled the Colonel away from a peaceful afternoon among his medals, 'that this invention is on quite different lines from anything I have attempted before. I will demon – er – strate it to you, Dedshott.'

The Professor climbed up on to a little platform with railings round it that stood before a machine which was chiefly composed of a big mirror when seen from the front, but which, when one peered round at the back, was seen to contain a generous helping of twiddley works, all ready to revolve in various directions at the slightest persuasion.

'When a penny is placed in the slot and the mirror is – er – looked into, the machine automatically produces a piece of poetry having some direct bearing on the person inserting the penny,' said the Professor.

'Bravo,' said the Colonel, expecting the worst.

'Splang!' the Professor put a penny in the slot.

'Whizz whiriririr pop pop popetty pop.'

The machine gulped down the penny and let itself go. After a few seconds of mechanical moanings, a long strip of paper came squirling out of a little trap door and wound itself round the Professor's ears.

'There you are, Dedshott!' said the Professor. 'Be good enough to read it.'

The Colonel almost found he wasn't good enough to get it all unwound, but at last the two of them held it down and read:

> Now I'm a professor,
> Both learned and wise,
> I have to wear glasses
> Because of my eyes.

T–B

But one pair of spectacles isn't enough
For inventing and other professorish stuff;
And so I have many
For different jobs;
Such as reading,
   and writing,
      and thingumibobs!
But really, you know, it's a tiresome affair,
Having five pairs of glasses, but goodness
   knows where . . .

I understand science,
Its 'etics' and 'isms'.
I know about Euclid,
Triangles and Prisms.
I speak every language from Greek to Patelf,
(The latter is one I invented myself.)
The toughest of problems,
I solve in a trice,
By mental contortions,
It's all very nice,
But I wish that I knew of some good formula
For finding out just where my spectacles are.

'Jolly good, my word!' grunted the Colonel, who reckoned anyone or anything who could arrange words so that they made sense and rhymed as well must be pretty clever. 'I'll have a basinful of that, by Jove.'

'Spang!' went the Colonel's penny and he stood rigidly to attention while the works went round.

Three yards of mechanical poetry shot out and the Colonel and the Professor nearly had it to bits trying to read it at once from different ends.

I don't command the Halberdiers,
The Grenadiers or Chiffoniers,

I've nothing to do with Auctioneers
Or Pioneers or Buccaneers,
I'm Colonel of the Cavaliers,
The Catapult, sir, Cavaliers.

I wouldn't be a Musketeer,
I'd hate to be a Chandelier,
An Engineer or Chanticleer
Would make me feel most insincere:
So I became a Cavalier,
A Catapult, sir, Cavalier.

Just then Mrs Flittersnoop arrived to say something but had no chance to get a word out before the Colonel and the Professor had her clamped in front of the machine and were looking for pennies. They had just discovered that all they had between them in the way of coins, apart from the Colonel's medals, which would have been a bit costly as penny-in-the-slot material, were two farthings, the counterfoil of a postal order, two weeks out of date, half a penny stamp and a native threepenny bit from the Diddituptite Islands, worth five new pence.

Mrs Flittersnoop was just about to fish in her purse and oblige with the loan of some of the laundry money, when a severely sizzly new idea caught the Professor a daisy one and he had the machine in bits all over the floor.

'I cannot understand why I did not think of this before – er – ah – Dedshott,' he said, with his mouth and one ear full of screws and spectacles. 'An obvious improvement. Poetry, Dedshott, should not be read, it should be – er – ah – um – read aloud.'

'Of course, what!' agreed the Colonel, wondering how anything could be read aloud if it wasn't read, but reckoning the Professor knew best, only not seeing how he could this time.

'A vocal attachment, Dedshott,' said the Professor over his shoulder, clanking about with the works. 'The poem to be recited by the machine as well as being delivered on paper.'

'Yes I'm sure, sir,' said Mrs Flittersnoop, who had begun to smell scorching and wanted to get back to her ironing before anything tragic happened to someone's best whatsname.

At last the Professor had it all worked out and fitted in and ground down and propped up.

'I think, Dedshott,' he said, 'that I owe it to myself to have some sort of public function to – um – demonstrate this invention. It is my first contribution to the cause of inexpensive entertainment. We must get the Mayor to open it.'

The Mayor of Pagwell didn't feel equal to opening a Branestawm invention. But finally the Professor nailed him down to the opening business by presenting his machine to Pagwell Corporation, together with five other sensational slot machines, each designed to give you the utmost excitement for the least money in the shortest time.

'The machines must go in front of the Town Hall, being in the nature of a public gift,' said the Borough Surveyor.

'They will obstruct the traffic,' argued the Chief of Police who obstructed the traffic a good deal himself when walking about, as there was plenty of him and he didn't think it dignified to hurry much.

'Put 'em in Pagwell Arcade and brighten the place up a bit,' said a councillor.

There might have been a lot of argument on the subject but fortunately there was a heavy question to be settled as to whether notices in the Pagwell buses saying that one must not spit on the floor entitled one to spit on the ceiling. So it

was hurriedly decided to put the machines in Pagwell Arcade, where they went very well against the imitation Egyptian pillars with early Welsh carvings.

The penny-in-the-slot poetry machine was supported by a sort of chorus of the other slot machines. There was one which gave you hiccoughs for a penny and took them away again for two-pence. Another, when tenpence was placed in the slot allowed you ten shots at a fierce-looking vase and let you take away the vase if you couldn't hit it. Fivepence-in-the-slot ice skating was another device. Here you put your feet into a pair of skates on the edge of a large saucer covered with ice and your fivepence made the ice go rapidly round while you stood still on it if you could. Most people couldn't, but falling off didn't entitle you to your fivepence back. The other two machines provided you, the one with a cup of tea, up your sleeve if you didn't unhook the cup and hold it under the spout quick enough, and the other with the loan of a complicated telescope through which you could admire the moon, if it happened to be night, but the Arcade was closed then, and if the roof hadn't been in the way, which it was.

The Mayor read out a long speech which he had brought with him by mistake and should have been let off at a meeting of the Ladies' Flower Guild. It contained references to 'these charming ladies' and 'always looking so sweet and flower-like themselves' which didn't seem quite to apply to the Professor's machines which he kept waving a hand at, or to the Professor, who kept bowing as it seemed polite, or to Colonel Dedshott, who was there behind all his medals, his ordinary working day ones and his best ones as well.

'I have pleasure in declaring the machines open,' finished the Mayor, getting into the right department at last, 'by inserting the first penny in the slot. Now let us see what Professor Branestawm's mechanical poet will have to say about me, ha ha ha!'

He picked up a new penny from a red velvet cushion held by the Beadle and placed it in the slot, standing well aside so that everyone could see the machine at work.

'There now I'm sure!' said Mrs Flittersnoop, who with her sister Aggie had managed to get right in the front row.

The machine whizzed and clanked. Then it began to chant,

'On a nice drying day, when the sun begins to shine,
I like to be out early with the washing on the line,

And I always think, when the things are blowing fine,
  It fairly makes you happy just to see them.'

'Something gone wrong!' grunted Colonel Dedshott,
wondering whether to smash the machine at once and be
done with it.

'But if the sun goes in, and it pours and pours and
  pours,' (went on the machine)
'And there's nothing else to do but take and dry the
  things indoors,
Oh, they steam on the walls and they drip upon the floors,
And it fair gives me the miseries to see them.'

'Well now, that's just what I always say, Aggie!' said Mrs
Flittersnoop.

It certainly was. Mrs Flittersnoop was right in front of the
machine. The Mayor, so carefully keeping out of the way,
had automatically kept himself out of the poem. The only
person the machine had reflected in its looking glass was Mrs
Flittersnoop.

Pong. A neat roll of poem shot out of the works and dropped at her feet but sister Aggie's dog had it to bits before she
could pick it up.

Then the Mayor, reckoning he had better do something to
cover up what he thought was his mistake, hastily fished
another coin out of his pocket and clapped it into the machine.

It wasn't a penny. It was a fifty penny piece.

The machine had never been treated so generously before.
It started trying to give the Mayor fifty pennies worth of
genteel poetry about himself but found it difficult owing to
only part of the Mayor being reflected in its mirror, along
with parts of dozens of other people.

'Now I the Mayor of Pagwell am
Municipal as any tram

> I clank along with penny fares
> And folk run up and down my stairs.'

This last bit was because a tram had gone by and reflected itself in the machine.

> 'While tasty sirloin I can sell
> Pork sausages and chops as well.'

A butcher gentleman had got in the way.

> 'Now pass along please, what's this here
> I'll have to take your name I fear.'

That was a policeman's hand trying to keep the crowd back.

Someone put a penny in the telescope machine and had a squint at the poetry machine through it. The machine sort of focused itself back through the telescope, got a wrong way round view of the person behind it, tried to do a bit of poetry in a mechanical whisper and accidently returned nine pennies splang through the poetry-giving-out-door. Some of the coins went down various drains but a few landed among the works of the other slot machines.

Immediately wholesale penny-in-the-slot pandemonium broke out in all directions with the poetry machine determinedly shouting hurried rhymes, some of which began to be slightly rude.

Colonel Dedshott, trying to make up his mind what machine to tackle first, received three cups of tea down the collar and one on the eyebrows. The Vicar of Pagwell and Mrs Flittersnoop were scooped up for a frantic helping of ice skating, while the Mayor received a present of a nice attack of hiccoughs but the machine ran out of coins before it could take them away again.

> 'There was a young man of Havannah
> Who spoke in a B.B.C. mannah,'

roared the poetry machine, going off into awkward limericks. Whizzy zizzy zizzy, went the Vicar and Mrs Flittersnoop on the ice.

Splash, splash, Colonel Dedshott had a hatful of tea with no sugar.

'I hic de-hic clare the hic machines closed-hic closed,' spluttered the Mayor doing his best.

Splash, whiz-z-z. 'Dear me this is most awkward!' Tut Tut. 'Stop the hic things.' Clank, whirr.

'A reckless young lady called Nan at a cafe had roast beef and bran. Then she found she'd no money, cried "Isn't that funny?" and taking her shoes off, she ran.' Whizz clank.

Tea poured out of the tea supplying machine and melted the ice in the skating machine so that the Vicar and Mrs Flittersnoop began to be whirled round in the dust. Colonel Dedshott wrenched the telescope off the telescope machine and hit the hiccough-giving machine such a one that it split in two and fifty-eight people had hiccoughs all together.

'By Jove, sir, hic what, ha ha hic hic,' panted the Colonel.

Professor Branestawm leapt at the poetry machine and pushed someone's umbrella into the works just as a councillor with an exceedingly high class name got in front of the mirror. The machine bellowed, 'The name of this gent is Fitzglossington,' then burst in a sheet of purple flame, possibly from the effort of making a sudden rhyme of such uncalled-for proportions and possibly due to the umbrella in the works.

Bong!

Then the fire brigade arrived, and everyone went home very damp, while all the old iron merchants in Pagwell broke out in bargain sales to dispose of the remains of the Professor's exterminated engines.

4

Ici One Parla die Languages

LANGUAGES, of course, were a strong point with Professor Branestawm. Unlikely languages, that is. He could speak the talk of the Diddlieuplite Islanders almost better than they could speak it themselves. He would have been quite at home talking to a Bigganlittle native apart from the fact that he would have had to go a long way away from home to find one. He knew at least five extinct languages, two of his own invention that nobody else could understand, as well as a special army sort of ordering about language he had picked up from Colonel Dedshott.

But when it came to everyday, ordinary languages like French, German and Spanish, the Professor was nowhere. His exhaustive and exhausting studies of unusual things left him no time for knowing about usual ones.

'Er – um,' he said to himself, turning the pages of a French guide book to Germany, with Spanish illustrations. 'There is, I fear, not sufficient time to learn these languages. I must invent something. Yes, yes, of course, that is exactly what I must do.'

Mrs Flittersnoop had just won a holiday abroad in a crossword puzzle in spite of the Professor having helped her with it.

'And if it wouldn't be troubling you too much, sir,' she had said, 'I'd take it very kindly I'm sure if you would come with me and give a hand with the foreign words you're so clever with. Not but what the holiday wouldn't do you good too, I should say,' she added.

A holiday abroad for Professor Branestawm! Excellent. It would give him an opportunity of studying the needs of foreign peoples in the matter of inventions. He might get valuable ideas. It would be most instructive. Yes, of course, he would go. And Colonel Dedshott would come too. Not that he agreed much with foreigners, but going abroad and being a foreigner himself would be rather jolly, what! The only abroad place the Colonel had been to was somewhere very tropical where the Colonel hadn't bothered to learn more than the native words for 'Do as I tell you or be shot at dawn,' leaving the natives to do the rest of the language learning themselves.

So now Professor Branestawm was in the thick of a most international invention.

'It is always an advantage in a foreign – er – country to be able to speak and understand something of the local tongue,' said the Professor, peering over and under various pairs of spectacles at Mrs Flittersnoop and Colonel Dedshott who had assembled for a demonstration on 'How to enjoy yourself in Foreign Parts'.

'In the usual way,' went on the Professor, 'one has to spend considerable – ah – time, and not a little – um – patience, learning the language of the place one proposes to visit.'

'Yes, I'm sure, sir,' said Mrs Flittersnoop.

'I have done away with all that,' continued the Professor beginning to pick up small pieces of machinery. 'Here we have Branestawm's Automatic Vocal Translator.'

'Bravo!' said Colonel Dedshott.

'This portion of the apparatus,' explained the Professor holding up a miniature saxophone-looking article with a box and some strings attached, 'is fastened over the mouth, the breathing being done as usual through the nose. Now,' he said, 'with the translator in position, you have only to press the button marked with the language you wish to speak, and continue to talk your own language. The apparatus will convert your speech into the language of the corresponding country.'

He fastened the machinery on to his own face and went on talking, pressing first the French button, then the Spanish, then the German, and so on.

The result was like someone trying to get foreign stations on the wireless and succeeding much too well.

Slodges of assorted Continental talk came pouring out of the translator accompanied now and then by a slight squeak as the machinery dealt with one of the Professor's rather

considerable words, some of which actually weren't trans-
latable at all.

'Marvellous, Branestawm!' gushed the Colonel, 'that'll
show those foreign beggars what's what, by Jove, yes!'

The Professor took the apparatus off and picked up a sort
of pair of smoked spectacles for wearing on the ears.

'Be good enough to put these on, Dedshott,' he said, 'and
see if you can understand what I am saying.'

The Colonel got into the hearing part of the translator.
The Professor clipped the talking part on again, pressed the
appropriate buttons on both lots and managed to make the
Colonel understand strings of high-class German that neither
of them knew a word of.

'In actual practice, of course,' explained the Professor,
'one wears both parts of the apparatus and is thus enabled
both to talk to and understand the people of any country.'

'There now,' said Mrs Flittersnoop. 'Whatever will they
think of next?'

The Branestawm-Dedshott-Flittersnoop holiday tour
abroad began very well. The automatic vocal translator
worked perfectly in Spain and France, though Mrs Flittersnoop couldn't get out of the habit of talking broken English
to foreign people, which came out of the translator as severely
fractured French and shattered Spanish. Colonel Dedshott
took the military precaution of carrying a book of useful
phrases as well as an automatic translator to make sure of
being understood. But the Professor sailed gaily through the
sights of every town talking more local language than the
inhabitants knew themselves. One Spanish Matador's
Secretary bought himself a dictionary after talking to the
Professor, and went home to brush up his own Spanish.

Then the party arrived in Germany.

'We shall first visit Cologne in the province of Rhineland, Prussia, situated on the left of the Rhine,' said the Professor, talking like a guide book through having read so many.

Outside the Cathedral the Professor stopped a highly German-looking gentleman in blue spats, and asked him the way to the Post Office.

'Take that thing off your mouth and perhaps I can understand what you've been talking about,' said the gentleman, who was English and wanted to know the way to the Post Office himself.

'Dear me,' thought the Professor, 'something seems to have gone – er – wrong with my translator.'

The Professor's hearing apparatus turned this piece of English into German, and the Professor heard it as, 'Können sie mir den Weg zum Postamt zeigen?' which was exactly what his speaking apparatus had just said to the blue spat gentleman when the Professor asked the same question in English. Nothing had gone wrong with it but the hearing part was adjusted to translate German into English and when English was spoken at it, it translated that into German. The Professor hadn't discovered that. When he and Colonel Dedshott and Mrs Flittersnoop spoke to each other their talking apparatus translated their conversation into German and their hearing machinery turned it back into English. Quite satisfactory.

'Can you show me the way to the Post Office?' asked the English gentleman in English. The Professor took off his translating machinery to inspect it. 'Do you know where the Post Office is or don't you?' demanded blue spats. Professor Branestawm stared at him and then at the automatic translator in his hands. Here was a queer state of things. He could understand German when he wasn't wearing the translator and couldn't understand it when he was.

'Really, that is most extraordinary,' he said. 'Rubbish!' snapped blue spats and stalked away to find the Post Office for himself, while an ornamental Cologne policeman came over to the Professor in case his translating machinery had anything to do with blowing up the Cathedral.

'Can you show me the way to the Post Office?' said the Professor brightly, forgetting to put on his translator.

Colonel Dedshott, who felt more at home with people in fancy uniforms, came to the rescue with his German phrase book.

'We want to find the Post Office, you know,' he said, and, opening his book, jabbed a military finger hurriedly on a piece of conversation that said, 'Kindly clean my boots and see that they are well polished,' The policeman gave a howl, snatched away the book, whizzed over the pages and pointed to a ticking-off sort of sentence about speaking more politely. But the policeman's finger was on the wide side, and the Colonel looked by mistake at 'These shorts are too fancy. Show me something plainer.'

'Ha!' thought the Colonel. 'Thinks he'll make fun of us because we're foreigners, what! Two can play at that game, by Jove, sir.' He showed the book back at 'Kindly be more civil or I shall report the matter.'

This happened to be exactly the sentence the policeman had been trying to show the Colonel, so he nodded his head rapidly to show that he approved. Colonel Dedshott thought he was apologizing and tried to come back to the question of being shown the way to the Post Office. But he handed the book the wrong way and his question got itself turned into a complaint about the price of fish. That started a terrific and most unlikely argument with not a word spoken on either side and replies getting more and more twisted up. 'Is there a hospital for cats in this town?' 'No thank you, I prefer to walk.' 'Bring me another cup of coffee.' 'Is the Museum open today?' 'Yes, if it is not too expensive.'

Meantime, Professor Branestawm had wandered off to look for Mrs Flittersnoop. But she was down by the river filling a medicine bottle with it because she was fond of eau-de-Cologne. The Professor went the other way and got himself lost among the colonnades of Zeppelin Street.

'Dear me, this is getting most confusing,' he muttered, as he ran round a pillar and nearly met himself coming round the other side. 'I must find the others at once. If we got separated like this, it may be difficult to – er – Pardon me, is this the way to Colonel Dedshott?' he said, stopping suddenly in front of a large lady with parcels.

'You must this way go and the third street on the right take,' said the lady, who didn't understand where the Professor wanted to be directed but was determined to be obliging.

'Er, thank you,' said the Professor.

'Please,' said the lady.

'Thank you very much,' replied the Professor.

'Please nicely,' said the lady, and they gradually got themselves tangled up in a non-stop performance of politeness which neither of them felt they could be the first to stop.

Down by the Cathedral, Colonel Dedshott's book of phrases had come to bits so that he and the policeman, each frantically determined to have the last word, had to chase about for stray pages with hoped-for suitably cutting replies on them.

'Is this your early closing day?' said a page the Colonel had grabbed as it floated by.

'No, it is too large, I take a smaller hat,' retorted the policeman after diving round a lamp-post.

The Colonel snatched up a page of advertisements by mistake and pointed dramatically to 'Do you suffer with pains after eating?' The policeman shot across the road, held up a string of four trams all tied together, and came back with 'Draw your chair up to the fire and warm yourself.'

Down by the river, Mrs Flittersnoop was having some rather scrambled conversation with the captain of a paddle steamer who wanted her to go for a trip down the Rhine.

Professor Branestawm and the parcel lady were still at their 'Bitte schön', 'Danke schön' business to which they had added a great deal of polite bowing and hat raising and were trying to get past each other, but found they both always stepped the same way.

Colonel Dedshott grabbed up a couple of dozen sentences about shaving water not being hot enough and accidentally pressed two or three extra buttons on his automatic translator.

'Confound it, sir, tell me where the Post Office is at once, by Jove!' he roared in Italian.

'You are a public obstruction causing!' shouted the policeman in German, which turned itself into Spanish and Chinese mixed as it went through the Colonel's hearing apparatus.

'No zank you, I do not care mooch for ze boats,' said Mrs Flittersnoop to the steamer captain.

'Oh, but surely you will one short trip go,' pleaded the captain. 'Only a little way to travel. A few yards perhaps. It is but jolly.'

Mrs Flittersnoop picked up her bottle of eau-de-Cologne river and marched determinedly away to find Professor Branestawm, with the steamer captain and his assistant steamboat sailors following.

The Professor and the parcel lady got away from Zeppelin Street by both deciding to go the same way. They arrived at the Cathedral still bowing as Mrs Flittersnoop and her steamboat escorts came round the other side of it.

Passers-by had begun to join in with Colonel Dedshott and the policeman in the useful foreign phrase showing and Post Office way asking.

'What size are these socks?' 'Don't believe you have a Post Office at all, my word, what!' 'Parlez-vous Français?' 'Do not the pavement obstruct.' 'Just a little trip across the river then.' 'Are these eggs fresh?' 'I do not want to take ze trip.' 'Si, si, Seignor.'

Sheets of paper changed hands and were rapidly shown round. Several sorts of languages flew about in assorted showers. Nobody could understand anybody else and didn't expect to. The Professor's translator fell off and was picked up by a German errand boy who had Irish relatives and picture postcards of Denmark. The automatic translator got out of hand and turned everything into very rude and low class Bulgarian slang. Five more policemen came to the rescue and were instantly engaged in silent papery arguments about laundry and cough drops. Two dear old German ladies were talking rapidly in non-existent languages through spare pieces of translator that had come apart.

Things began to get threatening. One of the policemen jogged Mrs Flittersnoop and made her drop her bottle of river. She pushed him away with her umbrella and he fell against the other policemen who went down in a row like skittles on top of Professor Branestawm and the parcel lady. Colonel Dedshott brandished someone else's walking stick and tried to clear a way to the nearest tram. Shouts of all kinds went up.

'Out of my way, by Jove! Confound it, what!' 'I will

everybody arrested have.' 'Ya, funny face!' Crash. Wallop. Dong dong. 'Wouldn't go near your Post Office now by Jove.' 'Will you not one small steamboat trip go?'

In another moment, the Professor, the Colonel and Mrs Flittersnoop would have been scooped up and done goodness knows what to. The situation was awful. Then a thunderstorm broke out. Rain poured down. The translating machines were struck by lightning and disappeared in pink dust and a cloud of bad language. The policemen put on enormous waterproof capes and disappeared round corners. Nearly everyone else parked themselves into a string of trams that went ding dong and shot off in all directions.

'My word, by Jove, what!' grunted Colonel Dedshott. 'A nice trip on the steamboat take,' said the steamer captain who didn't mind thunderstorms and was still there. He hustled them politely on board, including the parcel lady who was too out of breath to say any more, presented Mrs Flittersnoop with a quart bottle of real eau-de-Cologne, went zoom zoom on his steamer siren, and off they went with a special German river steamboat band playing special German river music.

'I shall not be – er – sorry to get back to Pagwell, Dedshott,' said the Professor, as they chugged along. 'Rather, by Jove, yes, what!' agreed the Colonel, who was dimly under the impression he had managed to fight a duel with the German policeman on horseback, with catapults, in the botanical gardens, being all muddled up after his confused conversation.

'I really think I like my holidays better at home, thanking you kindly, sir, I'm sure,' said Mrs Flittersnoop when they were safely back in Pagwell. 'These foreigners do take on so.'

She poured out the Professor's tea and cut him a slice of her special currant cake with jam in the middle, marzipan on top and cherries round the edge.

'Er – ah, danke schön,' said the Professor thinking he might as well be frightfully funny for once.

'Bitte schön, I'm sure, sir,' replied Mrs Flittersnoop, being a bit quick on the uptake.

'Danke schön,' said the Professor and it was three quarters of an hour before the Professor managed to say the wrong word and finish the unfinishable politenesses

5

Professor Branestawm and the Babies

PROFESSOR BRANESTAWM looked at the baby over the top of all five of his pairs of spectacles.

The baby looked at the Professor over the top of his mum's back. His mum patted him on his own back.

'I – ah – hullo,' said the Professor.

'Burp,' said the baby, blew a small bubble and added, 'Ge-e-e-e.'

'That's got it,' said mum, who in fact was Mrs Flittersnoop's sister Aggie's cousin Ada from North Pagwell, who had brought her nice new baby to show off.

You might not think there was anything in that to set the Professor off on a new invention. But it was one of those days, and before Mrs Flittersnoop and cousin Ada were half-way through their fourth cups of tea, the Professor was nine-tenths of the way through a highly twiddley device for helping babies to burp better.

'You know how one gets the gurgley noises in the water pipes at times,' he said to Dr Mumpzanmeazle, who had called in to see that the baby was in good running order. 'Well, it's the same kind of thing. A baby's – um – ah – windies are caused by a sort of air lock in the pipes.'

'Of course,' said Dr Mumpzanmeazle, waving his stethoscope about and knocking the Professor's glasses into the gluepot, which fortunately contained only a clean handkerchief the Professor had put there by mistake instead of in his pocket. They were in the Professor's inventory. The walls were covered with little pink doggies and blue bunnies which Mrs Flittersnoop had stuck there to help the baby atmosphere.

And on the bench stood the Professor's Baby Burper its own self. It looked like a toy steamroller with three funnels, but not very much like one.

'When you press down this lever,' explained the Professor, 'an electronic movement is set up which releases the – er – wind in the baby's . . .'

'Exactly,' cried Dr Mumpzanmeazle, who knew all about wind in baby's plumbing. He shot off into a great deal of doctorish talk about tubes and digestive thingummies. The Professor's head began to go round and round, just as Colonel Dedshott's always did when the Professor explained things to him.

'You follow, Professor?' asked the Doctor.

'Quite, quite,' said the Professor, who hadn't been listening as he had just thought of a sort of optional extra attachment for his invention, to make it cure hiccoughs with a further attachment, five times larger than the machine itself, for preventing milk boiling over.

Dr Mumpzanmeazle shot off to see somebody about some spots, and in walked Mrs Flittersnoop's cat, who had just finished a kingsize saucer of milk. 'Brr, brr,' said the cat, jumping up on the bench and rubbing himself against the Baby Burper, which promptly went 'Tweet, tweet'. The cat said 'Burp.' Then as he didn't agree with having his windies brought up without his permission, gave the machine a dirty look and stalked out with becoming dignity.

The Professor had arranged to demonstrate his Baby Burper at the Pagwell Baby Clinic. He wrapped it up in some fancy paper covered in pansies and baby ducks, left it on the hall table, came back for it and left his hat on the hall chair. Then he came back for that, forgot where he was going and finally arrived at the Pagwell Baby Clinic by getting on the wrong bus, thinking he was going to Pagwell Zoo, which happened to be the right bus for going to Pagwell Baby Clinic.

'We shall be most interested to see your invention, Professor,' said the Matron, smiling with all her teeth at once and folding her hands over her waist as far as they would go, which wasn't very far as she was considerably on the large side.

'The babies have been fed?' inquired the Professor, unwrapping his invention. Dr Mumpzanmeazle had impressed on him that it couldn't bring up a baby's windies, if he hadn't got any windies to bring up. 'Best time is just after a feed,' he said. It was this being concerned with feeding time that had almost led the Professor to the Zoo. Thank goodness he didn't get there because of what might happen if you make an enormous elephant burp.

'This wheel,' said the Professor, holding up the invention with the air of someone selling cough mixture, 'can be turned according to the size, duration and strength of burp required.'

'According to the size of feed consumed,' added the Matron nodding to the row of mums who had come to have their babies de-burped.

'And here,' went on the Professor, 'is an adjustable thingummy arranger for using the machine on grown ups after such things as – er . . .'

'Christmas parties and summertime outdoor blowouts,' said one of the mums.

'Precisely,' said the Professor. He aimed the machine at the first baby in the line, and pressed the lever. 'Tweet,' said the machine and, 'Burp,' said the baby. Everyone was delighted.

'Saves all that back slapping,' said another mum, who had had triplets and been given rather an overdose of back-slapping herself in consequence.

'Burp, burp, burpetty burp,' The Professor moved down the line with his invention. The demonstration was being a roaring success. Then he put down the Baby Burper while he blew his nose. A little boy with red hair, who had got his head stuck in a pink plastic toddy pot that didn't go with it at all, came crawling along and bumped into the Burper,

which promptly resented it. Tweet, tweet! Burp! Plop!
Plonk!

The little boy burped a grown-up size burp, the toddy
pot flew off his head and landed on a little girl who was
playing with a blue teddy bear and giving no trouble up to
then. 'Gurururur“urg!' she shouted and threw the teddy
bear at the Professor, missed him by half a room width but
scored a direct hit on a tray of tea a nurse was bringing in
for the mums.

'Crash, sloshety bang!' Clinical china was all over the
place. Steam went up. The nurse who was scared of the
Matron at the best of times, leapt into a play pen and
tried to hide under a heap of striped woolly balls. One
baby who was rather a late feeder pulled the top off her
feeding bottle and poured the contents over the Professor's
head.

'Pwouff!' he gasped, blowing valuable vitamins all over
the linoleum.

Then the Baby Burper really got out of hand.

'Burp burp, double burp, burpy burpetty burp!' all the
babies broke out in windie-upping. The Professor made a
dash for his machine and fell over a set of triplets who were
burping in waltz time.

The Matron opened her mouth to give severe orders but it
was immediately filled with high quality double sterilized
cotton wool thrown by a rather elderly baby who had
climbed on to the mantelpiece to get a better aim.

'Tweet tweet tweetie tweet,' went the Baby Burper, careering round the clinic with all levers pressed.

Burping broke out among the mums, who seemed to do it
even better than the babies. Soprano burps and treble burps
and contralto burps came rolling out. It sounded like a
Wurlitzer organ with energetic hiccoughs.

'Oh dear!' groaned the Professor, 'and I thought this was going to be such a nice quiet little invention that couldn't cause any uproar.' He clutched his five pairs of spectacles and tried to catch his machine.

'Stop this at – burp – once,' exploded the Matron.

Out in the street Colonel Dedshott was striding past on his way to a Regimental Tea Party of the Catapult Cavaliers, when a window of the clinic burst open and someone shouted, 'Help . . . burp!'

'By Jove, what!' exclaimed the Colonel deciding that Regimental Tea Parties must give place to rescuing people who needed help. 'Coming, my word, what!'

He dashed up to a door but it was marked 'Nurses only.' The Colonel's military mind instantly rose to the occasion. He dashed into a drapers shop that happened to be standing by and bought a nurse's cap and apron.

'To the rescue!' he cried, and with the apron on upside down and the cap tied on top of his Catapult Cavalier special dress hat, worn only for Regimental Tea Parties, he pushed open the door and rushed up the stairs.

'Burp burp burpetty burp!' a machine gun fire of windies met him. Seven mums tried to drape themselves round his neck. The baby on the mantelpiece opened fire with highly absorbent cotton wool balls.

Tweet tweet tweet.

Burp burpetty bang pop burp.

Down below two policemen looked up at the noise.

'I never did hold with these clinic places,' said one.

'Nor me neither,' said the other and they went off to find a nice quiet burglary to attend to.

'Rescue!' roared Colonel Dedshott brandishing his catapult. He looked wildly round at the assortment of burping babies. 'Ha, diddums then, by Jove!' 'Stop it there, ickle sweetie pie!'

For once even Colonel Dedshott was defeated. For how can even the bravest soldier contend with armies of babies? What can you do with an enemy that giggles and burps when you threaten him? What indeed!

'Help, Dedshott!' gasped the Professor from under a set of babies who were crawling over him with rattles waving.

Colonel Dedshott took aim with his catapult at the burping machine that was trying to climb up the Matron's leg. Plonk, he missed. The bullet bounced off the floor and hit the fire alarm bell.

'Clang-a-lang-a-lang!' yelled the bell.

'Tweetie tweet tweet,' squeaked the Baby Burper.

'Burp.' 'By gad, sir!' 'Help!' 'Burpie burp.'

Then the Matron slipped on some vitamin-activated ointment someone had spilt on the floor, and sat on the machine, which gave an agonized squeal and went flat.

Instantly the burping stopped. The mums grabbed their babies while the grabbing was good. Colonel Dedshott grabbed the Professor. They shot down the stairs just in time to meet the Great Pagwell fire brigade, who weren't needed for any fires but came in very handy for getting the Professor and the Colonel away from the battlefield.

So Colonel Dedshott arrived on the fire engine almost in time for his Regimental Tea Party, which meant he was in time for the cake but didn't have to eat bread and butter first, which the army is usually very strict about soldiers doing. But as he had forgotten to take off the nurse's apron, he nearly got himself mixed up with the washing up.

And Professor Branestawm was delivered safely home to Mrs Flittersnoop, a bit out of breath. 'In future I shall – er – avoid babies,' he gasped, collapsing into a chair which collapsed as well because it had only three legs and was waiting to be mended. 'Babies, I feel, are – er – somewhat dangerous.'

'Yes indeed I'm sure, sir' said Mrs Flittersnoop. She helped the Professor into a more complete chair and went back to the roly-poly she was making for dinner, which would probably be quite capable of producing a burp or two itself without the help of any sensational inventions.

But it was a jolly good job Professor Branestawm was never likely to have any babies of his own, who might need servicing, so to speak. Because the Matron of the Pagwell Baby Clinic definitely went off him in a big way after the hoo-haa his invention had caused, and whenever she met him in the street she stared across the street as if she hadn't seen him. But as he almost certainly would be too soaked up in a new invention to notice her, nothing really mattered much.

6

The Unexpected Tale of Professor Flittersnoop

PROFESSOR BRANESTAWM was walking down Pagwell High Street. And he looked extremely odd. He had buttons on his coat instead of the usual safety pins. His trousers were smartly creased right down the centre instead of sideways all over the place. His tie was neatly tied and he had his hat on the right way round. He looked nearly as elegant as a whole packet of new pins done up in a gift wrap.

Nobody would have recognized him. Nobody, that is, except his old friend, Colonel Dedshott of the Catapult Cavaliers, who was used to spotting not-done-up buttons on soldiers on parade and things like that. He penetrated the Professor's disguise in a moment.

'Branestawm, my word, hullo what!' he cried. He got off his horse, which he was riding for a treat. 'Going to a party or something?'

'Oh – ah – hullo, Dedshott,' said the Professor. 'You are surprised at my – er – um – somewhat strange appearance no doubt. It's a new invention of mine. You must come round tomorrow and I'll explain. I can't stop now, I'm on my way to lecture at the Pagwell Science Institute.'

He shot off down the road in the direction of the Library, in mistake for the Science Institute. But as it was really at the Library he was supposed to lecture, things were better than they seemed.

'Ha hrrmph!' said Colonel Dedshott, wondering what sort of an invention could make the Professor look so unprofessorish. He cantered off home, to wait until tomorrow when he would hear all about it from the Professor and probably not understand any of it.

Ding dong ding dong, clang bing a ding dong! The Professor's specially invented alarm clock went off. It sounded rather more like Robin Hood's wedding in technicolour than an alarm clock. But it woke the Professor most definitely up, which ordinary alarm clocks sometimes found it a bit of a job to do.

'A-a-a-a-h,' yawned the Professor. 'Oh bother, time to get up. This getting dressed business is such a waste of time. Doing it every morning and then un-doing it again at night. Why doesn't somebody invent . . .'

He got the answer to that question with a noise like ten squeaky sewing machines trying to beat eggs, followed by assorted pops and mixed bangs as the getting-you-dressed machine he had invented and forgotten about put him rapidly into his clothes, which it had pressed during the night. It brushed him down, brushed him up, washed his face, combed his hair, cleaned his teeth with a special rotary toothbrush and pineapple-flavoured toothpaste, polished his shoes and then left off with a satisfied sigh as if someone had carefully let the air out of a balloon.

'Ha, yes, of course. I invented that,' said the Professor. 'Clever of me, and it works splendidly.' He went downstairs, forgot about his breakfast and became all soaked up in a new invention for straightening curly bananas.

Mrs Flittersnoop, who had been staying with her sister Aggie for a few days, finished the last bit of washing up the Professor had left. It wasn't much really because he used only one plate, one cup and a spoon for everything, though she was a bit cross because he had put the little weeny teapot for one in the cupboard where the large visitors' teapot should have been. Then, pushing a nice cup of tea and a round of toast through the inventory window, where it got mixed up with sliced straightened bananas, she went up to make the Professor's bed.

'There now!' she exclaimed when she saw the getting-you-dressed machine. 'If it isn't another of the Professor's inventions he's been at while I've been away. I wonder if it's a machine for making the bed.' She pushed a little lever very gingerly, thinking there would be no harm in getting the bed made without having to do it.

Of course, she ought to have known better, did Mrs Flittersnoop. Her having housekeepered for the Professor ever since goodness knows when. And in two seconds she did know better this time. But two seconds is about half an hour too long to take to know better where the Professor's inventions are concerned, they being a bit on the hasty side.

Squeaketty squeaketty popetty pop, boing, bzzoing wallopetty smack, puff puff! Mrs Flittersnoop found herself in bed, while her best blue and white spotted dress and all her other clothes were industriously pressed and put away in the machine. The Professor had arranged it so that the machine not only got you dressed in the morning but put you to bed very considerately at night.

'Goodness gracious!' Mrs Flittersnoop tried to exclaim. But the machine popped a large sweet into her mouth, rapidly read half a page of a very scientific story at her and put out the light, which made no difference as it was daylight.

'Oh, glumph, ym ym, glop!' gasped Mrs Flittersnoop. She sprang out of the bed, swallowed the sweet, dashed into her room and hurriedly put on more clothes including her second-best blue and white spotted dress, which was exactly the same as the one the machine had got inside it, but not quite so smart.

Only just in time. Rat tat, Colonel Dedshott was knocking at the door, ready to have the new invention explained to him. When Mrs Flittersnoop opened the door he thought she didn't look quite so neat and tidy as usual. This was partly due to her not having entirely recovered from the attentions of the getting-you-dressed machine and partly due to the blue and white spotted dress being her second-best. For a moment the Colonel thought the Professor's invention for making him look smart had something, but goodness knows what, to do with making Mrs Flittersnoop look not quite so smart. But by then the Professor was five eighths of the way through explaining his banana-straightening machine and Colonel Dedshott hardly had time to get his thoughts sorted out before his head began to go round and round as usual, only this time rather faster than usual.

'Of course, the bananas have to be peeled first,' said the Professor, 'otherwise the resistance co-efficient of the peel operates counterwise to the straightening effect of the – er – straightener.'

'Marvellous!' gasped the Colonel, wondering how on earth bananas could turn the Professor out looking like a tailor's dummy got up for a heavy party.

The Professor, of course, had forgotten about the getting-you-dressed machine again. He had found that thinking about two inventions at once was apt to cause unheard of things to happen, though of course they were all too probably likely to happen even if he thought of no inventions at all, which he was too clever to do.

'Hrrmph!' said the Colonel on the way home. 'Now I suppose he'll write a book about the influence of fruit on people's dress or something. I don't know how he does it, my word I don't.'

That evening the Professor, still thinking about banana-straightening, forgot about the getting-you-dressed-and-putting-you-to-bed machine. So he undressed himself in the ordinary way by hand, and got into bed leaving his clothes absolutely everywhere.

Next morning 'Ding dong, etc.' went the wake-up chimes and, oh good gracious! Poppety flump, whiz, the Professor was rapidly dressed in Mrs Flittersnoop's best blue and white spotted dress, with trimmings, because those were the clothes the machine had all pressed and ready from the day before.

The Professor didn't notice anything. There are some things even a Professor can't do, and thinking about best blue and white spotted dresses that don't belong to them and straight and curly bananas, all at the same time, is absolutely one of them, as any professor will tell you if you ask him. Anyway he was in too much of a hurry to go out and buy some very long skinny screws for his banana machine even to wait for breakfast. He picked up a sausage off the table and was off to the ironmongers before Mrs Flittersnoop could stop him.

'Oh deary, deary good gracious me!' she cried, wishing she had stayed at her sister Aggie's. 'There he goes, all got up in my best blue and white.' She guessed that had something to do with the getting-you-dressed machine because she had become slightly quick at guessing things about the Professor's inventions, so as to be prepared when something drastic was likely to happen, which it nearly always was. 'I must do something to stop him indeed I must, or goodness knows what people will think.'

She hurriedly rang up Colonel Dedshott, who immediately organized a handful of Catapult Cavaliers to spread out through the streets of Pagwell, head the Professor off and bring him safely home. 'You'll know him by the blue and white spotted dress and five pairs of spectacles,' barked the Colonel.

'Try the ironmongers first!' shouted Mrs Flittersnoop down the telephone, not knowing the Colonel had already rung off and was getting his horse out to join in the hunt. Then, reckoning that the housekeeping must go on, never mind what, she set off in her second best blue and white spotted dress for the Pagwell Supermarket.

The Catapult Cavaliers were, of course, very good at fanning out through places because of their military training. But they had rather mixed ideas of where Professor Branestawm might have got to. Some fanned out round Pagwell Park where a cricket match was occurring which they felt

the Professor might just possibly be looking at and which they rather wanted to look at themselves. Others fanned themselves into a cinema where there was a morning performance, feeling that even if the Professor wasn't there, the time wouldn't be wasted as they wanted to see the film themselves. They were very resourceful, were the Catapult Cavaliers. Still others thought the Professor might be resting in Pagwell Gardens or watching the barges whiz by on Pagwell Canal, and they fanned themselves all round those places. And a few of them, having no idea at all where the Professor was to be found, fanned themselves out through the streets of Great Pagwell, diligently inspecting the scenery for signs of the Professor, particularly those parts of the scenery which were young and pretty and wearing mini skirts, just in case they were blue and white spotted ones.

On the way to the ironmongers, Professor Branestawm met Dr Mumpzanmeazle. He was on his way back from a little girl whose mum thought she had exaggerated measles, but which turned out to be spots of her lipstick the little girl had been trying to make herself look special with.

The Doctor saw at once that something was wrong with the Professor, without listening to his chest or giving him a thermometer to suck or making him say 'ah' or anything. He was mighty good at spots, was the Doctor, even blue and white ones.

'Whatever are you wearing that for?' he said, guessing the Professor didn't know. 'Come to my surgery and have a cup of coffee.'

'Dear me!' said the Professor, over his third cup of coffee and tenth custard tart. He was hungry from having had no breakfast, except the sausage, which he had tried to put in his pocket anyway. But Mrs Flittersnoop's best blue and white spotted dress didn't have pockets so the sausage fell by the wayside so to speak and was appreciatively munched up by a spare dog. 'Dear me!' he said. 'I didn't know I had a suit like this,' which of course he hadn't.

Then he explained his getting-you-dressed-and-putting-you-to-bed machine to Dr Mumpzanmeazle though even he couldn't explain how it got hold of Mrs Flittersnoop's dress.

'This is how it operates,' explained the Professor, finishing the Doctor's custard tarts by mistake and drawing complica ted diagrams on an already fearfully complicated chart of a red, white and blue man which showed you how people's muscles worked.

'Here is the trouser remover, presser and replacer,' said the Professor, drawing concentric circles round the chart's legs. 'This is where the jacket is hung up, any missing buttons re – um – placed,' two triangles and an oval on the chart's shoulders. 'A reversing lever here,' two dots on the chart's nose, 'enables the machine to undress one at night instead of dressing one in the morning. There is also – er – provision for turning socks right way out, arranging a shirt the right way – um – up, a necktie un-tier and re-tier, a bootlace dis-entangler and a woolly vest putter-oner.'

Dr Mumpzanmeazle listened carefully and his head didn't go round at all, not even half way. He had got used to hearing complicated scientific explanations when he was studying to be a doctor. He could understand the thickest descriptions and soon made short work of long words.

'Excellent, my dear Professor,' he said and at the bottom of the chart, which now had levers and springs and trap-doors instead of muscles, he wrote. 'To be taken twice daily, morning and evening' in the proper doctors' writing which nobody but chemists can read.

He thought the machine was a very good idea. He was always having to get up at ridiculous times of the night to go dashing off to people who were either frightfully ill without notice or thought they were, or to inconsiderate ladies who would go having babies before breakfast.

'Can't you make me one of these things?' he said. 'Be a great help in my practice.'

So the Professor said, 'Yes, yes, of course,' and off he went, wearing the Doctor's second-best raincoat to hide Mrs Flittersnoop's best blue and white spotted dress, which it didn't do entirely, the Doctor being rather given to shorty raincoats while Mrs Flittersnoop definitely favoured longy dresses.

Mrs Flittersnoop was in Pagwell Supermarket, trying to make up her mind whether it was cheaper to get a Family Size packet of soapflakes with sixpence off and a free bar of chocolate; or a Giant Size packet with nothing off, but coupons for saving up to get fish knives at half price; or four Large Size packets at rather more than three quarters price tied together with three tubes of toothpaste for the price of two.

Suddenly she was surrounded by three Catapult Cavaliers, two of whom took an arm each and escorted her with forcible politeness out of the Supermarket while the third marched behind in case she got away.

Of course they thought she was Professor Branestawm. You could hardly blame them. There was the spotted blue and white dress the Colonel had told them to look for. And there were at least two pairs of spectacles. One was the pair Mrs Flittersnoop always wore for looking at sensational bargain prices in supermarkets and the other was a pair of sunglasses she was going to buy for sister Aggie who was on the brink of

going off for a seaside holiday and expected rather a lot of
sunshine.

'How dare you!' cried Mrs Flittersnoop, stamping on the
Cavaliers' feet with her heels, which they didn't feel anything
to speak of because her heels weren't very sharp and their
boots were considerably thick. 'Let me go this minute.'

'All right, Professor Branestawm, no need to take on so,'
said the right hand Cavalier.

'You're in good 'ands, sir,' said the left hand one.

'You come with us and we'll see you're all right, Prof,'
added the marching-behind one.

'I am not Professor Branestawm,' protested Mrs Flittersnoop, putting on the sunglasses on top of her own spectacles
and so making herself look rather much like him.

'That's all right, sir,' said the right hand Cavalier, wink-
ing at the others. 'But you come with us just the same and
get your own clothes on instead of that dress, which don't
really suit you like, if you understand me, Professor.'

Mrs Flittersnoop immediately stopped seeing red and
began to see daylight, of which there was certainly a great
deal about, as they were now out of the Supermarket and in
Pagwell Square.

'Listen to me, young man,' she said, going all practical and determined. 'I'm Mrs Flittersnoop, Professor Branestawm's housekeeper. He went out this morning wearing one of my dresses by mistake. It was to do with one of those inventions of his. If you're looking for him you'd best start at the ironmongers.'

At this the three Cavaliers looked at each other and they began to see large quantities of daylight too. There was a bit of army sort of talk between them and plenty of explaining talk from Mrs Flittersnoop. Then they all began to laugh.

'Dear oh dearie me!' said Mrs Flittersnoop. 'It's the first time three young men have wanted to take me out at once, yes indeed I'm sure.'

And as they were just outside the Great Pagwell Ye Olde Bunne Shoppe, they decided to go in and have ye olde coffee and bunnes together.

'But what about the Prof?' said one of the Cavaliers.

'Oh, he'll be all right,' said Mrs Flittersnoop. 'The ironmonger, where he went to buy screws, will have seen what's wrong and he'll be home by now. And if he's damaged my best blue and white spotted dress – this being my second best if you see what I mean – I can always get another at Ginnibag & Knitwoddles' Sale.'

Of course the Professor had got home safely, though it was with the aid of Dr Mumpzanmeazle's raincoat and not with the ironmonger's help. And when Mrs Flittersnoop arrived back he was straightening bananas quite happily in his inventory, still in her best blue and white spotted, which was still as good as new, and quite undamaged, unlikely as it seemed.

So all was well that ended not too badly. But Dr Mumpzanmeazle had an absolute time of it with the Professor's getting-you-dressed-and-putting-you-to-bed machine, which would keep getting him up at three in the morning and then putting him straight back to bed again whether any patients wanted their temperatures taken or not.

7

An Apple for the Teacher

IT was Mrs Flittersnoop's sister Aggie's little girl, Esme, who really started it all. She'd read somewhere that in America children always take an apple to school for the teacher.

'Mum!' she cried. 'Mum, can I take an apple to school for teacher?'

Mum said all right, it was nice of her to think of it. And she wrote an order for the greengrocer for a 'pound of apples,' spelling it with one 'p' by mistake, which was a bit awful of her only she was thinking about the washing.

'Well, thank you, dear,' said the teacher when Esme turned up next morning with a big red apple. 'Thank you, that is sweet of you.' She couldn't stand apples much, really, but of course she wasn't going to say so. 'I can give it to Willie,' she thought. That was her little brother, who loved apples but liked them green, though they sometimes gave him tummywobbles.

'Mum,' said Elsie Baker, the ironmonger's daughter, when she got home. 'Please can I take an apple to school for teacher?'

'Well yes, I suppose so,' said her mum. 'If you think she'd like one.'

'Esme did,' said Elsie. 'So why can't I?'

Well of course, there isn't really an answer to a question like that, or if there is, Elsie's mum couldn't think of it. So next morning Elsie arrived at school with a slightly bigger and redder apple than the one Esme brought.

'How very kind of you,' said teacher, looking at the two big red apples rather nervously. 'Thank you so much, but you shouldn't.'

Next morning everyone in the class brought a nice big red apple for teacher. There were forty-five children in the class and the forty-five big red apples made the classroom look like Harvest Festival.

'Oh thank you, you really are too kind,' said the teacher, goggling at the apples, which looked even bigger and redder

than they really were because she wore rather strong spectacles. She began to work out frantic sums in her head to see how long it would probably take her brother Willie to get through this lot.

By the following Monday morning Esme's grand and generous idea had spread right through Lower Pagwell School. Every teacher had from thirty to forty nice red apples on his or her desk. And as there were ten classes in Lower

Pagwell School, that made roughly three hundred to four hundred nice big red apples to be eaten, given away or otherwise disposed of.

Tuesday came and with it another three or four hundred nice big red apples. By the end of the week the apple harvest at Lower Pagwell School had nearly reached two thousand. Weak cries of 'Thank you so much, dear!' and 'Oh how very kind of you!' and 'What a dear, thoughtful little boy (or girl) you are!' sounded through all the classrooms. And murmurs of 'You really shouldn't!'

'If only they really wouldn't,' groaned the teachers.

But they would, and they did.

Several thousand nice big red apples and more coming in at several hundred a day.

The teachers hurriedly called an apple meeting.

'Can't we tell the children to stop bringing them?' said one teacher.

'Oh dear dear no, we can't do that!' said the Headmaster. 'It would hurt their feelings.' He was a frightfully kind headmaster and hated hurting children, even if they didn't do their homework.

'What about Professor Branestawm?' said a teacher. 'Perhaps he could invent a way of solving the problem.'

So Professor Branestawm was sort of un-plugged from a vivid invention for a new kind of television that gave you three programmes at once, one upside down, and switched on to apples.

'Your – er – problem is really two problems,' he said to the teachers, changing his spectacles about to see which they looked best through.

'First is the problem of how to dispose of the apples given to you. Second is the problem of how to stop the children bringing the apples. If we solve the second, the first problem will no longer exist. Now,' he said, warming up a bit and ticking points off on his fingers, finding he hadn't enough fingers and borrowing a handful of the mathematics teacher's. 'Now, we could cut off the supply of apples to Pagwell; we could perhaps abolish apples altogether.'

'No, no!' cried the Headmaster. 'We can't deprive people of apples. Tut tut no! Apple a day keeps the doctor away, my dear Professor.'

'Well, I don't know,' said Dr Mumpzanmeazle, who had come to the meeting in case anyone fainted and wasn't at all sure he wanted to be kept away by apples. 'Do we really need apples all that much?'

Professor Branestawm waved the objection aside and showered spectacles all over the mathematics teacher, like runaway fractions.

'Of course, we need only abolish the apples as they are received by the teachers,' he said. 'Or possibly devise a means whereby the – er – apples could be returned into circulation so to speak.'

'So that the same ones would keep going round and round,' said a geography master, who was used to going round and round places himself.

'But,' protested a chemistry teacher, 'the apples would gradually become over-ripe, go bad and become a menace to health.'

'That's the trouble with apples,' said Dr Mumpzanmeazle, who couldn't quite forgive apples a day for keeping doctors away.

'Have the goodness to go away,' cried Professor Branestawm, gathering up his spectacles and waving them at the teachers. 'I can feel some ideas coming on.'

But as the meeting was at Lower Pagwell School it was the Professor who had to have the goodness to go away and thank goodness he got home to his inventory before the ideas came on really seriously.

He invented an apple abolishing machine that could be installed in the schools and dispose of the apples. But it was forty foot long and weighed eight tons. He invented a special kind of disappearing apple that would vanish after being presented, but it was square and coloured purple with yellow dots, which made it look a bit unlike an apple. He invented

apples with legs that could be trained to run back to the shops again, but they smelt highly disagreeable and had no traffic sense whatever, so might have got run over on the way.

Then a little boy who went to Upper Pagwell School had tea with his special chum, who went to Lower Pagwell School.

'Mum!' said the Upper Pagwell schoolboy when he got home. 'Can I take an apple to school for teacher like Bobby does?'

Soon Upper Pagwell School was doing three thousand apples a week, because it was a bigger school than Lower Pagwell.

'This is terrible!' cried the teachers. They were being appled out of their homes. They had apple pie and apple pudding and dumplings and stewed apples and apple fritters, but nothing could keep pace with the plague of apples. The cupboards and wardrobes were full of them. They had to wash outside because the bathrooms were packed with apples to the ceiling.

The North Pagwell School came in, followed by Pagwell Gardens, Pagwell Green and East Pagwell.

The Pagwell greengrocers ran out of apples five times a week. Urgent orders were rushed to Covent Garden market. Special apple lorries went roaring all through the night, carrying the big red apple cargoes to the Pagwells.

The apple shortage spread. Soon you couldn't buy a nice big red apple for love nor money anywhere except in the Pagwells.

Little Pagwell Primary School knocked up five hundred apples a week and Professor Branestawm replied with a gas-fired reciprocating apple-disintegrator.

'Something must be done!' declared the Headmaster of Pagwell Gardens School, who was a bit older than the other headmasters and thought he ought to set an example.

'Ah, Miss Frenzie!' he exclaimed, and rang up the Pagwell Publishing Company, where Miss Frenzie, a lady with wildly waving hair, was employed to think of brilliant ideas for extraordinary books.

'Hullo!' said Miss Frenzie, in a very sweet voice. 'How nice to hear from you, Headmaster, what can I do for you?'

The Headmaster explained all about the awful apple awkwardness. 'And I wondered if you could think of some way of er – er – ' he finished.

'Delighted,' roared Miss Frenzie. 'How about "The

Pagwell Apple Recipe Book or seven hundred ways of dealing with apples"?' She was mighty quick at thinking of things, was Miss Frenzie.

'Splendid!' said the Headmaster who would have been quite satisfied with one way of dealing with apples.

'What's all that noise?' asked Lord Pagwell, at the Pagwell Book Company, shaking a severely choice chocolate out of a long skinny box and wishing there were more left. He was trying to work out his pocket money in new pence and couldn't hear himself think for the shouting.

'It's Miss Frenzie talking to Pagwell Gardens School about a new recipe book,' said someone.

'Well ask her to use the telephone,' said Lord Pagwell, calming down because he reckoned Miss Frenzie's new cookery book was going to make him a lot more pocket money, which he didn't at all mind having.

Professor Branestawm was travelling slowly along Pagwell High Street, on foot, trying to invent a special kind of computer that could subtract multiplying apples from themselves, and by dividing the answer by the number of apples first brought to school, let there be no apples at all left. Suddenly from across the road came a glad cry, 'Professor Branestawm!' And Miss Frenzie came hurtling across in front of a bus, that stopped so sharply all the passengers were shot up in a heap at the end irrespective of how much fare they'd paid.

'Professor Branestawm, my dear man, just the person I wanted to see!' cried Miss Frenzie, taking no notice of the greeting the bus driver was shouting at her. She had an armful of enormous pieces of cardboard, printed with vivid pictures and even more vivid words describing the apple recipes for her book. They were all tied loosely together with a piece of inadequate string, that broke as she reached the Professor. Instantly the street was full of original apple recipes of all kinds.

'Oh dear,' panted Miss Frenzie, giving chase to 'Hungarian Apple Charlotte' and 'Grandma's Double Decker Apple Pie' as they sailed across the road, running before the wind.

'I – er – ah – allow me,' puffed the Professor, grabbing at 'Roast Apples and Pork Sauce' and 'Apple Jitters', which should have read Fritters, missing it and treading on 'Apple Kicks'. A greengrocer's cart ran over 'Apple Pancakes à la Mode' and would have squashed it as flat as one only it was as flat as that already; and 'Savoury Apple Soup' nearly went down a drain.

'My dear Professor,' panted Miss Frenzie, having gathered the runaway recipes together somehow. 'You must come with me to Pagwell Gardens School. I have a wonderful idea for solving the apple problem and you will be most helpful. Quick, get a taxi.' She looked around wildly, spotted a black motor car, wrenched the door open, pushed the Professor inside, and fell in on top of him, nearly smothered in recipes.

Unfortunately it wasn't a taxi, it was the Mayor of Pagwell's car. But fortunately the Mayor's chauffeur was going home to lunch in it, somewhat illegally, while the Mayor attended a banquet in aid of distressed solicitors.

'Pagwell Gardens School,' cried Miss Frenzie, frantically sorting the recipes out from the Professor.

As they drew up at the School, the Headmaster was just sitting down in his study to a hurried lunch of pork chops and pink blancmange, when he saw the car through the window and thought it was the Mayor paying a civic visit.

'Good gracious!' he cried, and with a mournful look at

the pork chops he gathered the tablecloth up by the corners and carefully put the whole lot outside the garden door.

'Hullo, Headmaster!' cried Miss Frenzie cheerfully, shedding recipes all over the floor. 'Here are the drawings for the recipe book and here is Professor Branestawm who is longing to help solve our problem.'

'Hum,' said the Headmaster, looking at the apple recipes and feeling hungrier than ever. Then he realized he needn't have drastically disposed of his lunch as it wasn't the Mayor after all. He rescued the chops and blancmange from the garden while Miss Frenzie went into renewed raptures over the recipes.

'I – er – think perhaps,' ventured the Professor, clashing his spectacles about a bit to get himself noticed, 'we might – er – alleviate this apple business by sending some quantities of them to a distant place.'

'Marvellous idea, my dear man,' cried Miss Frenzie.

'How *do* you think of them? I know where we can send them,' she went on, not waiting to hear how the Professor could think of them. 'An old boy-friend of mine has a farm at Nether Blasthope. He can send them to market with his other things. I'll get my secretary to fix it.' She was on the phone to the Pagwell Publishing Company in three-quarters of a second. 'Violet,' she said, 'phone all the local schools and tell them to send their apples to Mr Farmer, who actually is a farmer, ha ha.'

'Righto,' said Violet, who was used to this kind of bursting instruction. She rang off, put her lunch back in the top right hand drawer of her desk and started telephoning. Nobody but the Mayor seemed to be getting any lunch that day.

'Well, that's that,' said Miss Frenzie. She scooped up the recipes, scooping up the Headmaster's pork chops with them and disappeared up the road, leaving the Headmaster, the Professor and the Mayor's chauffeur extremely uncertain where they were or what was happening.

But oh dear. In the excitement Miss Frenzie had forgotten that Mr Farmer's farm was one of those that are absolutely sprinkled with enormous cows and not the kind that grows rows and rows of fruit. After three days' supplies of apples had nearly submerged him, Mr Farmer had the bright idea of sending them to the Pagwell greengrocers' shops as he knew they were short of apples.

So the apple problem looked, just for a while, like being solved. But alas, no. Another frightful problem stuck its nose up. The same lot of apples was now going round and round, from the shops to the pupils, from the pupils to the teachers, from the teachers to Mr Farmer, from Mr Farmer back to the shops and so on round and round, like Colonel Dedshott's head when the Professor was explaining something. But after a few days of the apple roundabout the apples began to go off. Not go off bang like fireworks but definitely off as apples, as they got riper and rottener, just as the Lower Pagwell chemistry master had foreseen.

Two hundred more apples a day at Pagwell-on-the-Hill High School. Professor Branestawm opened fire with a set of internal combustion apple-abolishers that abolished one another.

That night, in the main road through West Pagwell, the midnight apple lorry from Covent Garden collided with Mr Farmer's apple lorry from Nether Blasthope. Nobody was hurt but the driver of the Covent Garden lorry went up in yells of anger.

'Ruffians!' he roared. 'Miscreants! Diddlers! Dishonest criminals!' He pointed to some of the apples that had fallen off Mr Farmer's lorry. 'Look!' he yelled. 'Those are mine. Albert's Prime Pippins. I know, they're marked with my trade stamp, a five sided square crossed out.'

Sure enough there was the mark on the apples. Albert's Prime Pippins had been delivered to the shops, bought by the pupils, given to the teachers, sent to Mr Farmer and were now on their tenth journey back to the shops. But Albert didn't know. He thought someone had been stealing his apples.

'Pardon me,' said Mr Farmer in a slightly well-off voice as he was that kind of farmer. 'Those apples were given to me and I am giving them to the Pagwell shops to ease the apple shortage. There is no law against that as far as I know.'

There wasn't as far as Albert knew either, so all he could do was shout 'Pah!' which is not a very satisfying thing to shout really, and climb back on his lorry.

Then Professor Branestawm invented Branestawm's Indestructible Plastic Apples.

'They will solve the – er – problem,' he explained to Miss Frenzie. 'Being plastic they will not go – ah – rotten.'

But of course that made things even worse, if possible, which by now it only just was. At least the ordinary apples could to some extent be got under control, by means of Miss Frenzie's Apple Recipe Book. But you can't cook plastic apples. You can't do anything with them except look at them, and everybody at the Pagwell Schools would rather have looked at anything than apples, plastic or otherwise.

On top of that the customers began complaining. One father who had tried to take a bite out of one of the apples his wife had bought, and which happened to be a Branestawm Plastic Apple, nearly broke his expensive false teeth and went ranting round to Mr Brown the greengrocer.

'It must be one o' they window display apples got in by mistake, so it must,' said Mr Brown and pacified his customer with a bunch of enormous grapes which, thank goodness, were real.

But alas! alack! oh dearie! dearie! tut tut! the frightful problem of the too, too many apples was still unsolved. Not even the combined substantial brain power of Miss Frenzie and Professor Branestawm could solve it. It wasn't any good calling in Colonel Dedshott and the Catapult Cavaliers either. Soldiers are no good against apples. The Mayor thought of declaring a state of emergency but didn't see how that would help as it would only mean sending policemen to guard the gasworks.

Schools at Pagwell Basing, Nether Pagwell and Pagwell Parva came in with four hundred apples a day between them. Professor Branestawm let fly with a heavy duty apple-inhibitor, with decoring attachment, that used apples for fuel. He invented seventeen more ways of dealing with apples, some of them dangerous, most of them considerably awkward and all of them impossible.

'This is ridiculous,' he protested. 'Here am I, a brilliant professor, who has invented world-shaking inventions, flummoxed by a mere thing to deal with apples.'

That night he had apple nightmares. He dreamt that an avalanche of apples had descended on the Pagwells and buried everybody, and woke up to find it was almost true. Thousands and thousands of apples were piling up in the schools. Mr Farmer refused to take any more as his cows were eating them and giving cider-flavoured milk.

Then one blissful day sister Aggie's little girl Esme was just off to school, when her mum said, 'You've forgotten the apple for your teacher, dear!'

'Oh, no thanks,' said Esme. 'We've done that. That's an old thing now, we aren't doing it any more.'

Gradually the apple aggravation subsided. The Pagwell Book of Apple Recipes broke all records. Professor Branestawm's Plastic Pippins adorned many a gracious sideboard and were carefully dusted every Tuesday. At last everything was back to normal.

'Thank goodness for that,' sighed the Pagwell school teachers.

The following Monday little Esme took an orange to school for the teacher . . .

8

The Rival Professors

A MOST unjust thing had happened in Pagwell. Another Professor had come to live there!

And what is more, this rascally rival had actually got himself taken on as a sort of high class lodger by Mrs Flittersnoop's sister Aggie.

'I don't think you should have done it, Aggie,' said Mrs Flittersnoop. 'Not but what you mayn't find it handy to pop along to me if the gentleman's inventions get troublesome like. But me being Professor Branestawm's housekeeper these many years, I don't call it playing fair, Aggie, to go a-taking in of the enemy so to speak.'

Then a heavy letter arrived for Professor Branestawm. It was headed in three sorts of coloured type with the words:

Professor GASKET BASKET
Inventor
Captain of Science
Master of Mechanics
and
Originator of Superemely Satisfactory Engines
for
Particular People.
Corporations Contracted with, Individuals Interviewed.

To Professor Branestawm.
Dear Sir,
    That is to say.
    I challenge you to an inventing contest in order to prove beyond

question the superiority of my methods over yours. Details to be arranged by Pagwell Council. Winner to receive the freedom of the town and a statue in the market place. Loser to leave Pagwell within twelve hours.

> Signed
>> Gordon Gasket Basket
>> Inventor etc. as hereinbefore stated.

The letter had such a shattering effect on Professor Branestawm that he ate his dinner in the ordinary way, with the mouth, instead of disposing of it into inkpots, waste paper baskets and pieces of invention as he usually did.

'Disgraceful!' exploded Colonel Dedshott when the Professor showed him the letter. 'Ignore his challenge, Branestawm. Above that sort of thing, what! Everyone knows you, by Jove. Fellow ought to be er – hum – pah.'

'I fear, Dedshott,' said the Professor, putting the letter behind the clock which immediately struck five too many and went back to last Thursday, 'that I must – er – accept this – ah – um – challenge. To refuse would be – er – tantamount to admitting defeat. No doubt I shall be able to devise some little thing to meet the – ah – occasion.'

Pagwell Council didn't like the challenge any more than Colonel Dedshott did.

'It seems to me that this is not a matter with which the Council should concern itself,' said the Mayor.

'The money people will pay for admission to the Town Hall would be useful for buying new drains for the High Street,' put in a Councillor.

'Why not get the Professor to invent new drains and get 'em free?' said another.

Then there was some complicated argument about giving the freedom of Pagwell as a prize because it would mean the winner could sit on the park deck chairs for nothing, have free dinners at the municipal cafés as often as his inside could stand it and speak to the Mayor without raising his hat.

At last the details were settled. The rival Professors were to set to work and each invent some sort of machine, engine or mechanical works for doing a domestic task such as washing up, beating carpets, cleaning grates and so on.

'We can't judge an inventing contest if one of the Professors invents a new kind of flower pot perforator and the other one makes a steam piano,' said the Mayor. 'It would be like doing a sum in elephants and apples and trying to get the answer in lemon cheese tarts.'

'Aye,' agreed the other Councillors except the one who was Headmaster of Pagwell College and often set sums like that himself.

The rules of the contest were briefly:

1. The inventors must demonstrate their inventions on the platform at Pagwell Town Hall on a certain date before an audience.
2. No smoking in the hall.
3. No money refunded.
4. The Council reserved the right to turn out anyone they thought proper, which was their way of saying they would turn out anyone they didn't think proper.
5. There would be refreshments.

'Well, Branestawm, good luck and all that, what!' roared Colonel Dedshott. 'What's the invention going to be, hey?'

The Professor decided to invent a machine for de-pipping grapes which, if it seemed awkward to invent, could probable be sort of smoothed off into an automatic pastry-board cleaner. But by the time he had it half done, it had become a slightly unruly cindersorter cum egg-whisk. And owing to lack of weeny screws or the use of too much wire of the wrong thickness, it finished up as a thing for mending punctures on steam rollers.

Then Colonel Dedshott helpfully pointed out that a steam roller mending equipment didn't come under the heading of domestic machinery. So the Professor turned the whole affair upside down, when three parts of it fell out and it would very likely have worked quite well as a boot cleaning engine. Only, he put back some of the grape de-pipping mechanism, did some fancy soldering, bent the ends, and made it into a kitchen gramophone for speaking recipes at the cook, with attachments for stirring things well for five minutes and taking three eggs as often as possible.

Meantime sister Aggie felt she ought to make up for harbouring the enemy so she did some amateur secret service work at the key-hole and came along to Mrs Flittersnoop with the news that the rival Professor was spending most of his time either playing the mouth organ or eating thick mincemeat sandwiches. She couldn't be sure which, either from the sounds she heard or the face movements she saw, possible because the keyhole needed blowing out.

Then Colonel Dedshott came round post haste on his horse which delivered him through the window to save him knocking or ringing.

'My word you know, Branestawm, have just had an idea, what!' he grunted. 'You must have protection. Rival Professor may be a miscreant. Supposing he sends people to smash up your invention. I will detail company of Catapult Cavaliers to surround house – investigate suspicious sounds and report to you hourly.'

'But,' said the Professor, who didn't like the idea of being disturbed every hour of the day and woken up every hour of the night to be reported to about sounds probably

made by hoarse pussy cats or drastic drippings on to tin roofs.

'Any attempt to tamper with your invention will thus be frustrated at outset,' went on the Colonel. 'Miscreants seized and shot at dawn without trial, by Jove.'

'Well – er – um – ah,' said the Professor, seeing visions of shot-at-dawn dustbins and other domestic furniture strewn over the garden. 'I have already – er – taken precautions.'

He led the Colonel to his inventory. In the middle of the floor stood an invention. A wow of a one. It had more cog wheels than any piece of machinery has a right to have all at once. Levers stuck out in all directions like little fingers at a polite tea party. There were numberless knobs and positively empires of switches.

'Marvellous!' gasped the Colonel. 'Best thing you've done by the look of it, Branestawm. All the more reason for precautions. I'll send orders to six and a half battalion at once.'

'This is not my invention,' said the Professor.

The Colonel looked at him sideways.

'Er – that is to say I invented it,' said the Professor, 'but it is not my invention all the same. That is to say it – ah – er – um – I shall not show it or rather – er – er – have the goodness to operate the machine,' he finished.

The Colonel pushed, pulled and twiddled everything. Nothing happened.

'An ingenious device I think, Dedshott,' said the Professor. 'You see the idea. Anyone attempting to – er – wreck my invention will naturally pick on this machine, which is nothing but a dummy composed of old inventions fastened together haphazard. I obtained the idea from Pagwell Broadcasting Company whom you may remember keep a roomful of – er – discarded machinery, in which they are in the habit of letting loose angry persons annoyed with the programmes who, having destroyed the – ah – contents of the room, go away satisfied that they have wrecked the works when actually they have done nothing of the kind.'

'Bravo!' said the Colonel rather weakly. Partly because the Professor's description of this sort of upside down kind of invention had made his head go round and round the wrong way and partly because he was disappointed not to be able to camp his Cavaliers out among the pansies and daffodils.

'It was the easiest invention I have – er – invented,' said

the Professor. 'Because, not having to work, it cannot possibly go wrong.'

Then the real inventing went on apace. Mrs Flittersnoop stood it as long as she could then fled from the house carrying a basket of groceries and two paper novels followed by ten kinds of hot smells and three sorts of scientific hammering.

Meantime sister Aggie found it no easier to put up with the mouth organ playing noise or mincemeat sandwich eating noise, whichever it was, from her Professor than Mrs Flittersnoop found it to put up with Professor Branestawm's inventing. So she left with the remains of Sunday's bread pudding in a clean serviette and set off to stay for a while with Mrs Flittersnoop. The two of them met in Pagwell High Street and decided to stay for a few days instead with their Auntie Sue, who kept Pekinese sort of doggies by the dozen and so was used to having people about the place.

The day before the great contest the Professor heard suspicious sounds in the house without the help of any Catapult Cavaliers.

'Um, as I thought,' he muttered. 'An attempt to damage my new invention. Hum, it is fortunate that I made the decoy.'

Muffled crashing noises came from the inventory.

'I hope I – er – made it reasonably difficult to smash, muttered the Professor, turning over.

Hushed clankings occurred. Thud, rattle, rattle, shush, bang.

The Professor grunted, turned over again and fell out of bed. By the time he had found his way in the dark, back into the right piece of furniture after attempting to finish the night, (a) in a half open drawer, (b) in the bottom of the wardrobe and (c) on the mantelpiece, all was quiet again.

The miscreants had done their work. But ah ha! Branestawm had been too many for them.

Next morning Professor Branestawm was round at Colonel Dedshott's house wearing one leg each of two pairs of trousers and three coats, two inside out and one upside down.

'Dedshott, come at once, tut tut, disaster, I fear. Most urgent.'

'Hey, what's that, by Jove?' grunted the Colonel, coming out of his newspaper with a rattle of medals.

'Miscreants have been!' wailed the Professor. 'They have stolen the real invention!'

Things were awful. The rival Professor and his hired rascals had either thought the decoy looked too inventish to be an invention or else they had been afraid of it. They had taken the real invention. Yes, yes, and the rival Professor was going to show it that very night at the Town Hall!

What could Professor Branestawm do? Send men to steal the other Professor's invention and hope it was better than his own? No. No. Professor Branestawm would win by fair means or not at all.

'Have to take the decoy along, that's all,' grunted Colonel Dedshott, when they reached the Professor's house. 'And trust to getting a chance to swap them over.'

But by the time they had managed to get the decoy on to the platform the audience were already wedged firmly in their seats. The Mayor was getting his speech ready, the rival Professor was standing fiercely by the stolen machine and nothing could be done but hope for the best, which the Professor and the Colonel did plenty of.

Pagwell Silver Prize Band were playing tastefully all the same tune, seated behind a row of plants because although they had highly elaborate and very prize tunics with acres of braid, they had no trousers except their ordinary walking-about ones, which didn't look at all musical.

The music stopped. Then the Vicar of Pagwell began a collection in aid of woolly vests for Chinese orphans but only got as far as three bent pennies and a button when the Mayor, who had forgotten about him, stood up and made his speech.

'Professor Branestawm as the challenged party has the privilege of demonstrating his machine first,' he finished.

'Play for time,' hissed Colonel Dedshott from behind a palm. 'Let the other fellow do his stuff first.'

'I do not – er – wish to take advantage of my opponent,' said the Professor. 'I forgo my privilege. He may begin first.'

There was a slight cheer at this which did very well to fill in the time taken by the Mayor to get unwedged from his seat which had gone up on a hinge when he stood up so that he had got sort of stuck in the works when he sat down.

'Professor Gasket Basket will begin then,' said the Mayor.

The rival Professor glanced triumphantly at Professor Branestawm. Then he pressed a lever on the stolen invention.

Nothing happened.

'Thank goodness,' breathed the Professor.

His opponent twiddled wheels.

No result.

'Perhaps the Professor will tell us what his invention is supposed to do,' said a Councillor.

After ten minutes of concentrated nothing the Mayor got up again and a box of chocolates Mrs Mayor had put on the edge of his seat went sailing up into the balcony to Mrs Flittersnoop as the seat swung up. But Mrs Flittersnoop had just changed seats with sister Aggie, though as they shared the chocolates it made no difference.

'We must give the competitor time to adjust the doubtless delicate machinery of his invention,' said the Mayor. 'Professor Branestawm, kindly show us your effort.'

Professor Branestawm mournfully pulled a lever on the dummy decoy invention.

Now whether the dummy invention had been a bit shaken up in its journey to the Town Hall or whether it was annoyed at being ignored and the real invention stolen instead, or whether it was that the Professor, when he deliberately invented a non-working invention, invented something wrong as usual, goodness knows. But the non-working invention worked.

It not only worked. It positively performed.

It juggled three Town Hall chairs in circles to the tune of 'The way you look tonight' which it played on its own levers, sounding like a sort of flat xylophone a semitone sharp. It shot round the stage cutting flowers and exposing the non-musical trousers of the prize band, made them into a bouquet, the flowers, not the trousers, minced them up small and cooked them into a square pie with green icing on. It had half the boards of the stage up to see if there was anything wrong with the drains and finding there weren't any it made the boards into a little watchman's hut with the words, 'Beware of men at work', written backwards on the front. It varnished as much of the Town Hall as it could reach, which fortunately wasn't much. It had one of the curtains down and started to run the bandsmen up some decorative trousers to match their tunics but ran out of stuff as second cornet was a bit wide round the centre. In fact this not-intended-to-work dummy decoy uninvention did almost everything except light work with a horse and van or taking in washing.

Cheers for Professor Branestawm went up. The rival Professor hit the stolen invention with a chair. The stolen invention turned on him and fastened him up in the watchman's hut the other invention had made.

Then the rival Professor gave in. He admitted he wasn't a Professor at all. He had come to Pagwell intending to challenge Professor Branestawm and win the contest by stealing the Professor's work without inventing anything himself.

Of course, he lost the contest and had to leave Pagwell by the next train, which was slow and bumpy and stopped at all stations, and in between as often as it could.

'I am afraid Professor Branestawm must be disqualified,' said the Mayor when things quietened down. 'Although his invention does remarkable things, hardly any of them could be called domestic.'

Which was true enough. So Professor Branestawm failed to win the contest his opponent definitely lost, thanks to the unexpected workability of an invention that had gone right by going wrong. Then Professor Branestawm was carried shoulder high to the refreshment room and stood more doughnuts and ginger beer than he ever thought he had room for.

Not getting the freedom of Pagwell didn't worry Professor Branestawm because he hardly ever sat in park deck chairs and never remembered to pay if he did; always had his dinner at home where Mrs Flittersnoop was handy to see that he ate some of it sometimes; and hardly ever spoke to the Mayor except by letter, where the question of hats on or off didn't arise. And the Pagwell stonemasons were delighted at not having to make a statue of him, owing to the scarcity of stone safety pins for fastening his coat and the probable impossibility of finding five kinds of transparent marble for his spectacles.

9

Peril at Pagwell College

A VERY tall, black spider, with too many legs, stood in the Science Room at Pagwell College. 'Pay careful attention,' it said, in a thin, lemon flavoured voice, 'as I shall require you to take notes later on.'

It was Mr Stinckz-Bernagh, the science master, in his black gown that was torn into spider-leggy strips at the edges. He was taking Form $3\frac{1}{2}$ in chemistry. There were five rows of assorted boys. Some were in Form $3\frac{1}{2}$ because they just couldn't make Form 4; others were there because they were a bit on the smart side and used to get the answers in Form 3 before the masters did.

'Please, sir,' said a fattish boy with sticking-out ears, 'will this make us into chemists, sir?'

'Certainly not,' said Mr Stinckz-Bernagh, whisking the torn ribbony ends of his black gown out of the way of a little gas flame that seemed to fancy them.

'What's it for then, sir?' asked a short, pale boy in long dark trousers.

Mr Stinckz-Bernagh stuck out his jaw and moved it about as if he were chewing nougat, which he wasn't; but it made him look fierce, which he definitely was.

'Everything is composed of chemicals,' he said, as if this answered the question. 'You are all nothing more than a few packets of chemicals.' He pointed a skinny finger at the boys. Before they had time to fancy themselves as packets of Pot. Chlor. Amm. Nit. and Sulph. Whatsit, the door flew open and a rather elderly schoolboy with a nervous face came in.

'Please sir, the Headmaster wants to see you in his garden,' he said. 'Professor Branestawm, sir, is there sir, please sir.'

'Ha!' cried Mr Stinckz-Bernagh. 'We shall continue this lesson later. Grizzlebut, stay here and keep order while I am away.'

He shot out, followed rapidly by the torn ends of his gown which only just escaped being shut in the door.

'Got any suckers, Grizzlebut?' asked big ears.

'Shut up,' said Grizzlebut. 'I've got to keep order. He said so.'

A long skinny boy with a lot of hair got up and went behind the desk. 'Now pay attention to the next experiment,' he said, sticking his jaw out to make himself look like Mr Stinckz-Bernagh, which it didn't anything much. He picked up a bottle. 'We have here a substance called . . .' He looked at the label, found he couldn't pronounce it and went on. 'A substance which we pour into this – this back answer,' he said.

'Retort,' said big ears. 'That's a retort, that's what that is.'

'Look here, you can't do that,' protested Grizzlebut. 'You aren't allowed to mess about with the chemicals.'

Long hair tipped the contents of the bottle into the retort. Back answer would have been a good name for it. It exploded with a bright green bang and several million stars.

'Coo!' shouted the class.

A clump of the stars landed in a little bowl of dirty powder. Whee, zizizizi pop boing! Tongues of flame shot out in all directions.

'Ooer!' cried the class. Grizzlebut seized a glass of water and threw it at the flames. They threw it back in the form of very sizzly steam. Then two or three jars of extremely quick-tempered chemicals resented all these goings on and blew up themselves, just to show that it wasn't only retorts and dirty powders that could do it.

Bang, boom, cracketty crash! Popetty fizzle boingngngng bong! The Science Room was full of smoke, fountains of coloured flame tore across the room. Long hair made a dash for the door, was beaten to it by half an inch by Grizzle-but and the rest of the class fell on them. Bongetty bong, swoooosh pow!

Firework displays were nothing to it. A helping of ceiling came down and a column of white hot goodness-knows-what started to build up in the middle of the floor.

The boys tugged at the door handle. But Mr Stinckz-Bernagh had locked the door to stop them dodging the rest of his lesson.

Fourteen feet of dark purple smoke descended on them.

'Help!' yelled the boys.

'Help,' cried the Headmaster, to Professor Branestawm, out in the garden, 'help with the gardening is what we are most in need of, er, I should say of what we are most . . . that is to say what we badly need.' He hurriedly straightened out his grammar in case anybody important was listening.

'Yes, of course, er – um – ah – exactly,' murmured the Professor, who was the only other important person there and he hadn't been listening. He was considerably occupied trying to fasten together a machine that looked something like an inside-out lawn mower with funnels.

'Labour-saving machines are the best means of coping with shortage of labour,' said Mr Stinckz-Bernagh, putting his hands behind him, rocking backwards and forwards on his toes and nearly falling into a pond occupied by a very disagreeable-looking fish.

Professor Branestawm turned a wheel and pulled a little
skinny lever. The machine stuck a small spade into a flower
bed, lifted up a dollop of wet earth and put it in the Headmaster's pocket.

'Gardeners are so difficult to get,' said the Headmaster,
shaking the earth out on to Mr Stinckz-Bernagh. 'They

find it more, ah, paying, I think the term is, to get employment at the new hygienic sausage factory.'

'Not to mention free hygienic sausages twice a week,' put in Mr Stinckz-Bernagh, flipping the wet earth over to the Professor.

'Now perhaps you will be good enough to demonstrate to us your gardening invention,' said the Headmaster.

'This is the geranium-planting-out gear,' said Professor Branestawm, putting on his demonstration spectacles. The machine dug a neat hole in the lawn and planted a feather duster, which the Professor had brought to represent a geranium, the real thing being a bit out of season.

Just then a window of the Science Room opened. It opened in fifty places at once and did it by firing all the glass out in little bits, like crystal confetti. Pretty, but alarming.

'Good gracious!' cried the Headmaster.

A sheet of flame accompanied by mixed bottles and exploding test tubes came out after the glass.

'The chemistry class!' yelled Mr Stinckz-Bernagh.

He tried to climb through the broken window but was instantly set on fire by a row of flaming thingummys and immediately extinguished by an explosion that blew his gown off.

'Dear, dear!' muttered the Professor, feeling that something had gone wrong somewhere but not seeing that it could be anything to do with his gardening machine, which was now happily digging fancy holes across the lawn.

'Branestawm, by Jove, what's up?' came a shout from the road. It was Colonel Dedshott, marching happily on his way to a grand reunion tea of old Pagwellian ex-Catapult Cavaliers, mostly over ninety.

Of course, the Colonel took it for granted it was the Professor's invention that had started everything; because the

Professor was definitely there and so absolutely was one of his inventions. And where Professor Branestawm and one of his inventions occurred simultaneously you could usually look out for bangy stuff. Only this lot didn't need much looking out for. It was making itself plentifully noticeable without any help.

Boom! Two red-hot desks came sailing through the air and landed on the rhododendrons.

'We must save the boys,' shouted Mr Stinckz-Bernagh. 'The boys! They're locked in the Science Room.' He tore round to the front entrance of Pagwell College. Colonel Dedshott tore after him. The Headmaster tore round in circles, trying to stop the Professor's hole-digging machine and do something about saving the boys, both at once, and succeeding only in treading on a highly prickly plant which promptly stuck needles into his sitting-down part.

'Help!' yelled the Headmaster. He shot off after the Colonel and Mr Stinckz-Bernagh, calling out Latin exclamations in a very educated voice.

'Save the boys!' shouted Mr Stinckz-Bernagh.

'Save the children!' roared Colonel Dedshott, who had read that somewhere.

'Save for the future!' advised a Pagwell Bank poster on the wall.

'Save fourpence!' screamed a packet of supermarket sausages in a shop opposite.

'God save the Queen!' squeaked an inferior gramophone someone had set off by mistake.

Smoke and stars, burning bottles and glowing globules came hurtling out of the Science Room window. Chemical catastrophe howled round Professor Branestawm's head.

'I really think this – er – chemistry business is taken too seriously at schools nowadays,' he said, shaking his head and switching the gardening machine over to digging up the Headmaster's prize dahlias, which it did rather well.

Swish! A two gallon jar of boiling acid shot past the Professor's left ear, disarranging his five pairs of spectacles.

'Tut, tut, this is most careless,' he cried. 'I really must make a complaint to the . . .' Slosh! A square yard of jelly sort of stuff flopped out of the window and a very unclean glass jar landed on the gardening machine.

That did it. No invention of Professor Branestawm was going to stand that sort of impertinence. The machine heaved up a shovelful of earth and three Class 1 dahlias and dumped them on the jelly.

Pale blue flame lapped out of the Science Room window.

The gardening machine slung a shovelful of earth through the window. The Science Room returned it red hot and smelling highly unpleasant.

'Dear dear, I must make some adjustment,' began the Professor. But his gardening machine had got its mad properly up and had no intention of being adjusted. It scooped up an entire bed of Gesiggieclokkie Grandiflora and slung it through the window. It followed this by half a ton of well-manured soil.

The Professor pulled the biggest lever he could see. It came off in his hand.

Twenty spadefuls of compost and a cubic yard of wet leaf-mould hurtled through the window.

Outside the Science Room door there was nearly as much energetic pandemonium as inside the room.

Mr Stinckz-Bernagh dived into his pocket for the key. His fist went clean through the pocket and the key went clanketty-clank down a grating.

Colonel Dedshott hurled himself at the door.

The boys inside screeched like a thousand parrots disagreeing with one another.

Smoke belched through cracks in the door. Flames came creeping under the door. The Colonel stamped on them and they crept back.

Out in the garden the Professor's machine threw the lawn through the window.

Floomph, phut plip wuff umph. The flames went out. The explosions stopped. The smoke very nearly cleared away.

The Headmaster with great presence of mind at last remembered his own bunch of keys, found the right one after only seven goes, and threw open the Science Room door.

The dirtiest-looking scrabble of boys he had ever seen, in his many years of boys connected with dirt of innumerable kinds, came out.

'Please sir, we sir, help sir,' they gasped.

But it was all right. No harm done that a few dozen hot baths wouldn't put right. Nobody hurt, except to the extent of a trodden-on half bar of chocolate and three partly used bullseyes rendered unfit for further service.

'I – er – am afraid my gardening machine has rather spoiled your garden, Headmaster,' said the Professor, after some sorting out had been done. 'Some substance fell out of a window on it and dis – ah – rupted the self acting reoscillating . . .'

'To blazes with the garden!' cried the Headmaster, which in point of fact is exactly where most of it had gone to. 'The boys are saved, that's all that matters. The place is insured. We can rebuild.'

'It was really time we modernized the Science Room,' murmured Mr Stinckz-Bernagh.

So one of Professor Branestawm's inventions actually

saved the situation by being put wrong by an outside disaster which it then put right.

Pagwell College was closed for two weeks, for repairs. This enabled Form $3\frac{1}{2}$ to be got fairly clean again by a set of extremely energetic mums and plenty of soap and water.

10

The Adventure of the Ha Ha Hazard

PAGWELL presented a most unusual spectacle one zizzy morning. All the inhabitants seemed to have cricks in their necks. Actually it wasn't a crick but a curiosity that was making them look so eagerly upwards.

High above, gliding in and out of the clouds like a sardine swimming in a bowl of pale custard, purred a sort of something. It was shaped like a flat teapot and coloured like a silver goldfish.

'That be one of Ezra Ozzletwozzie's pigeons a broke loose again,' said one of the Pagwellians.

'Naw, now, that it don't be,' said another, 'more like as your Willie Wimble has been letting off of rockets and left one up there.'

'It is probably not there at all you know,' said Mr Stinckz-Bernagh, the science master from Pagwell College. 'The minute atoms of foreign matter in the atmosphere reflecting the sun's rays obliquely, in conjunction with cloud forms and pendant moisture, have probably produced an appearance that is not fact.'

That, of course, sounded like a piece of conversation from Professor Branestawm. And, as a matter of fact, Professor Branestawm had something to do with it. The silver something was his latest invention.

'Branestawm's Stratospheric Limousine,' he had explained to Colonel Dedshott. 'It has all the speed and – er – um – efficiency of the aeroplane with the long – er – staying-up powers of the airship. Yet there is no danger of punctures, if you follow me, Dedshott, for the entire outer casing is made of a special substance which I discovered partly by accident.'

'Marvellous, by Jove,' said the Colonel.

'Er, yes, quite,' said the Professor absently, draping his five pairs of spectacles round his neck and fixing on a pair of very bay window looking goggles trimmed with blue fur, which promptly slid down and nestled round his chin like an unexpected beard. 'I am not at — er — liberty to reveal the exact formula, but I may say that it contains, among other things, powdered aluminium, sealing wax, a little of Mrs Flittersnoop's home-made lemon cheese and a certain quantity of soda and milk. It is first composed in the form of a paste, moulded to shape and left to harden. When hard it is so, ah, um, hard that nothing will cut it.'

'Amazing, my word, what,' said the Colonel. 'What does it go by, elastic or something?'

'The propulsion is effected in several ways,' said the Professor, opening little lids in different parts of the machine. 'The chief motive power is a small steam engine which uses steam made, not from water, but from a mixture of ginger beer and some medicine which Dr Mumpzanmeazle prescribed for me the last time I had some sort of illness. Then there is an, er, supplementary clockwork motor which operates its own rewinding gear so that it never runs down. And in case that should fail we have – er – pedals. I hope you ride a bicycle, Dedshott?' finished the Professor.

Colonel Dedshott hoped he would never ride anything so unmilitary.

And now the Professor's Stratospheric Limousine was well on its first flight filled with the Pagwell Gas Company's favourite gas. The Professor was navigating while Colonel

Dedshott stood by with a hammer in case anything went wrong. The Mayor of Pagwell was guest of honour and sat in the exact middle of the machine to keep it balanced. Dr Mumpzanmeazle had left instructions with his patients not to get taken ill for a day or so and was busy unrolling bits of bandages and rolling them up again to make sure they were all there.

And, of course, there was Mrs Flittersnoop. There would also have been sister Aggie, sister Aggie's Bert, sister Aggie's little girl, sister Aggie's mum and dad and several connected-up relations. But there wasn't room for any more people and refreshments as well, so sister Aggie and company were left behind in favour of three packets of sandwiches, ten bottles of raspberry flavoured lemonade, half a pork pie and six almost hard boiled eggs.

'Ha, er, um, most instructive,' said the Professor. He leaned out to see how Pagwell canal looked from above, and dropped one of his pairs of spectacles down the funnel of a nice new steamer, which promptly puffed them up again, wrapped in a basinful of coloured smoke.

'Ha, most delicious, by Jove,' grunted the Colonel sitting in a corner and beginning on the sandwiches.

'I must say I appreciate your inviting me on this trip,' said the Mayor, not daring to move in case things capsized, 'but I feel it is my duty to warn Professor Branestawm that it is probably against the bye-laws to fly over Corporation property.'

'Hm, it seems we're passing over the gasworks,' said Dr Mumpzanmeazle taking his own temperature and getting it wrong.

It wasn't the gasworks, it was a packet of gorgonzola cheese sandwiches Mrs Flittersnoop had just unwrapped.

'Won't you come and have some refreshments, sir?' she

asked. 'You'll be tiring yourself out, I'm sure, sir, standing up steering the handles all this time.'

'Shall I take a turn at the helm, Branestawm?' cried Colonel Dedshott, getting ready to come over all nautical, or aeronautical, whether it was the military thing to do or not.

'I could steer for a little while myself if you like,' offered the Mayor staying where he was.

Dr Mumpzanmeazle took a long drink of some of his own medicine by mistake for lemonade and decided to write his prescriptions differently in future.

The Stratospheric Limousine gave a beautiful lurch as the Professor let go of everything and turned round.

'Oh my goodness, deary me,' gasped Mrs Flittersnoop, dropping the almost hard boiled eggs, only two of which bounced.

'Get down sir, whoa there!' roared the Colonel, starting to talk horsey talk which made no difference.

The Professor grabbed a doughnut and wedged it into part of the works.

The Stratospheric Limousine went purring along as smoothly as a Pagwell Tramcar. No! smootherly.

'The machine is fitted with automatic operating self steering and navigating gear,' said the Professor. 'It is now adjusted to operate without ah – attention.'

He sat down to help the Colonel with the sandwiches, though he didn't need much help except with one which the Professor had made and which contained red flannel instead of meat.

The Mayor of Pagwell sat as still as his own statue on top of Pagwell Town Hall.

'Will you have a sandwich, Your Worship, sir?' asked Mrs. Flittersnoop. She prodded one at where she thought his mouth was, but the machine gave a little sort of curtsy and the Mayor received a mouthful of ham and tongue in the eye.

Then they all settled down to a sort of up in the air sit on the floor kind of party with refreshment-having and story-telling. Colonel Dedshott told them all about when he was in different foreign places, but the Mayor was so busy getting ready to tell them how he played golf without digging any grass up, and Dr Mumpzanmeazle was so taken up preparing to explain how somebody once came out in the wrong sort of spots, and Professor Branestawm was so absorbed in thinking how satisfactory it was to have an invention go along so nicely, and Mrs Flittersnoop was so occupied handing round the refreshments and trying to have some herself without seeming impolite, that the Colonel's stories would have been entirely wasted if it hadn't been for the fact that he enjoyed telling them.

'And the natives were charging down on us from one direction, by Jove,' went on the Colonel. 'A herd of wild elephants were charging up from the other direction. A tiger was crouched on a branch over our heads and three snakes were coiled at our feet ready to strike. We had run out of ammunition. What did I do, sir? My word, yes, what did I do?'

'I just took my mashie and put the ball right on the green in less than fifteen strokes,' said the Mayor, who had begun his golf story in case the Colonel soon came to the end of his adventure stories.

'And that made me think that he couldn't possibly have meazles because the spots were the wrong colour, but I knew it couldn't be influenza because that has no spots, or shouldn't do,' added Dr Mumpzanmeazle.

'But the counterweight system is so adjusted that should

the differential gearing not function automatically no appreciable difference in stability will be noticed,' said Professor Branestawm, going on about his invention.

'I don't mind if I do, thank you kindly I'm sure,' said Mrs Flittersnoop going on with the sandwiches.

'Ran the other way and left the elephants to trample on the snakes while the tiger attacked the natives,' grunted Colonel Dedshott.

'With a dash of quinine and a pink pill twice a day,' added the Doctor.

'Seventy-five strokes each and only five more holes to play,' put in the Mayor.

'Unless reversing gear is employed,' said the Professor.

'Well, just one more,' said Mrs Flittersnoop.

Purr, purr, purr, on went the engine.

'Throwing spears straight into the hole with a little liquorice powder mounted on a camshaft but only half a glass,' went on the conversation, getting more rapidly assorted every second.

Purr purr, whrrr pip pip. 'Lost my gun, by Jove.' 'Just a thin slice.' Buzz buzz. 'Different sized cogwheels.' 'The spots were no bigger.' Whiz-z-z. 'You follow me, Dedshott.' 'Took my niblick to it.' Puff puff. 'Yes I'm sure sir.'

Suddenly the Mayor, who had got to a part of his golf story where his opponent had beaten him, stopped and said:

'It seems to have got a bit dark, don't – er – doesn't it?'

'Fog, by Jove,' grunted the Colonel.

Fog it was; thick as rice pudding.

Presently a dark shape loomed up ahead.

'Whoa, halt, hard a starboard there,' roared the Colonel.

Professor Branestawm pulled everything in sight, including Colonel Dedshott's whiskers and the Mayor's leg.

The Mayor collapsed on top of Mrs Flittersnoop and the

remains of the sandwiches. The machine grated against the dark something. Professor Branestawm frenziedly threw out mechanical grapplers and automatic anchors and self-acting catch-holders.

'Looks like a statue of some kind,' grunted the Colonel.

Professor Branestawm gingerly opened the door and let in a couple of bathfuls of fog.

'Ah, most satisfactory,' he said peering about. 'It is a statue we have come up against. It seems that in the, ah, fog we have gradually lost our altitude and, er, come down, apparently in Pagwell Square. I seem to recognize the general appearance of the stonework.'

'Everyone climb out in an orderly manner,' commanded the Colonel. 'No pushing. If we go carefully down the statue on to the pavement we can arrange for the disposal of the machine when the fog lifts.'

They clambered out one by one on to the statue.

Suddenly the Mayor gave a yell.

'Stop, hold on, for goodness sake!' he cried. 'Back to the machine. Quick, awful ahh-h-h-h!'

'What's the matter?' asked Dr Mumpzanmeazle.

'I recognize that statue,' panted the Mayor, clinging frantically round his own neck so to speak. 'It is the statue of me on top of the Town Hall. Over a hundred and fifty feet up in the air. Gracious me what an escape! If we had stepped off we should have been dashed to pieces.'

'Back to the machine,' snapped the Colonel.

But the machine had broken adrift and vanished into the fog. They were stranded, clinging like flies to a cold stone-work, but much worse off because they hadn't got sticking on feet like flies have, except the Mayor who had trodden on one of Mrs Flittersnoop's jam tarts.

Thank goodness Dr Mumpzanmeazle had his bandages

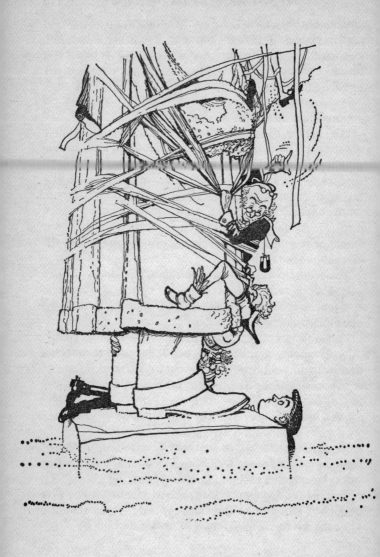

with him. After a lot of shouting directions to each other and not obeying them and a great deal of not letting go with one hand until they had two other hands and five feet firmly planted on the statue, they managed to tie themselves to the statue with the bandages.

Presently a clock struck. Bong.

'One o'clock,' said Dr Mumpzanmeazle.

'Eh, not necessarily,' said Professor Branestawm. 'It may may be, er, half past one, or indeed half past anything. We shall have to wait until it strikes again and even then if it strikes one again it may be, er, one o'clock or half past one because the ah previous stroke may have been half past twelve or one.'

'Pah!' snorted the Colonel.

Suddenly a head appeared below them, looking over the edge of the statue.

'We have, ah, been stranded here from a flying machine,' explained the Professor.

'Have the goodness to help us down your ladder at once,' said the Mayor.

'What ladder?' asked the head. 'I haven't got no ladder, guvnor. I've come to clean the statue like the Town Clerk said for to do, ready for it to go into the garden.'

'Ah, now I understand,' said the Mayor, 'it's the eighth of November, isn't it?'

'Aye, that it do be,' said the head. 'Statue do have been brought down from top of Town Hall for the garden.'

'What's the man saying?' asked the Professor, not understanding anything and feeling that it shouldn't be he who didn't understand things.

Just then the fog cleared away and they saw that they were clinging frantically to the statue of the Mayor that was standing flat on the pavement.

'Good gracious, by Jove,' cried the Colonel.

'Well I never, indeed sir,' said Mrs Flittersnoop.

All was well. It was the day before they were due to have a new Mayor in Pagwell, and that meant a statue of the new Mayor would go up on the Town Hall and the statue of the last-time Mayor had been taken down to be set up in the Municipal Garden of Honour. It was full of rows and rows of statues of once-were Mayors, but they all got on very well together and there was never any quarrelling.

'Well I must say, I'd rather see those adventures on the pictures than be in them, as you might say,' said Mrs Flittersnoop back home safely among the ironing.

The Professor's machine went whizzing on and on all by itself and was eventually identified as an unidentified flying object on its way to the moon.

11

Professor Branestawm's Christmas Tree

THERE had never been a Christmas party at Professor Branestawm's house before. Because the Professor was always so immersed in thinking about new inventions he never had time left to think about old customs. But this time the Professor was absolutely going to have a Christmas party, because he had invented a present-giving invention.

'I have always thought, Dedshott,' said the Professor to the Colonel, 'that the, er, traditional Christmas tree offered possibilities for, um, development,' by which of course he meant it could be interestingly fiddled about with.

The Professor swung his new invention round and the Colonel got a daisy one on the ear from a sticking-out part of the machinery.

'My idea,' said the Professor, 'consists of a purely automatic Christmas tree, fitted with a mechanical present distributor coupled to a greetings-speaking device and a gift wrapping attachment so that the, er, recipients receive their gifts suitably, um ah, wrapped up and accompanied by a Christmas greeting.'

He pulled a lever, pressed some buttons and twiddled a twiddler.

Pop whizzetty chugg chug. 'Good King Wenceslas,' sang the machine. 'Look out!' cried the Professor. A highly-decorative parcel shot out of the tree and landed on the Colonel's lap accompanied by a hearty 'Happy Christmas!' from the tree and 'By Jove, what!' from the Colonel.

'Jolly clever, my word,' he grunted. 'How does it work, eh?'

The moment he asked the question the Colonel wished he hadn't. He knew what would happen. The Professor would erupt in complicated explainings that would made his head go round and round. But this time it was all right. The Professor didn't explain anything. He came over all coy and said, 'Wait until my Christmas party, Dedshott.'

The Professor's party started off all nice and ordinary, apart from the fact that it took place in November because the Professor couldn't wait to show off his invention. The guests arrived with presents for the Professor.

Mrs Flittersnoop gave him a sweet little rack with five hooks for his five pairs of spectacles, which was meant for keys, but anyway the Professor hung his coat on it and collapsed the whole thing.

Colonel Dedshott weighed in with a paper weight made to look like a small cannon which made you feel you had to wait for it to go off though it never did.

The Mayor presented a photo of Pagwell High Street, in which he had a shop, in a green plush frame with gilt corners.

The Vicar handed the Professor a tastefully bound volume of his own sermons, autographed in mauve ink with ecclesiastical squiggles.

Sister Aggie's little girl was given a packet of toffee to give the Professor but she ate it on the way and gave him instead a sticky kiss on the forehead, which helped to keep his spectacles on. The postman brought a collection of used stamps with something wrong with them which made them much more valuable than they ought to have been.

'Er, ah, thank you,' said the Professor. 'Now come this

way please.' He led the way down the passage, into the kit-chen by mistake and nearly into the gas cooker and eventu-ally after much pushing and excuse-me's they all got packed into his study where the automatic mechanical Christmas tree stood.

'Here is the present distributor,' said the Professor, point-ing to a row of eager-looking levers. 'They are labelled with your names. All you have to, ah, do, is pull the lever with your name on.'

'Marvellous!' cried the Colonel.

'Shall I declare the tree open?' said the Mayor and the Vicar, both at once. Then without waiting for an answer they both coughed and, in very high class voices, said, 'I have pleasuah in declaring the tree open, hrrrmph.'

Soon levers were being pulled, the machine was clanking away, the air was full of Christmas music and hearty greetings and the crash of paper parcels being excitably unwrapped.

The Mayor got a pair of silk stockings and a bottle of lavender water, which were really intended for Mrs Flitter-snoop, because the Professor had got the names on the levers muddled up.

'Now that's what I call real kind,' cried Mrs Flittersnoop, then she said 'Oh!' in a rather pale voice when she found she had got a packet of corn cure and a tin of tobacco shaped like a pillar box, which should have gone to the postman.

Sister Aggie found herself with a box of cigars. The Vicar had a china doll with no clothes on. Colonel Dedshott's present was a yellow bonnet with imitation cherries on it. The Pagwell Library man got a packet of large square dog biscuits and wondered if they were a new kind of book.

'I fear there has been some mistake,' murmured the Vicar. 'May I be permitted to exchange this charming gift for something more suitable?' He pushed the china doll into the machine and pulled one of the levers. At the same time the Mayor and sister Aggie pushed their presents back and started pressing not-meant-to-be-pressed buttons, to change their presents.

'No no no!' cried the Professor, clashing his spectacles.

But he was too late. The automatic Christmas tree evidently resented having its presents returned. It rang out a burst of Christmas bells that sounded like a fire engine, emitted a cloud of dirty green smoke, shouted, 'Merry Christmas on the feast of Stephen!' and shot out of the house and down the road.

'After it!' roared the Colonel, who reckoned he knew how to deal with this situation.

They all tore after the machine that was shouting a mixed version of 'The Twelve Days of Christmas'. Colonel Dedshott drew his sword and rushed at it. The machine took it away and returned it gift wrapped.

'Five golden things,' sang the machine, careering down the road, giving out presents and Christmas wishes right and left. Three little boys with a November the fifth Guy who were asking for pennies got instead a parcel of files and screwdrivers that were the Professor's Christmas present for himself. A lady coming out of a supermarket was presented with the Vicar's china doll and a yard and a half of 'The Holly and the Ivy' sung out of tune.

'Dash round the other way and cut it off,' shouted the Colonel to the driver of a steam roller. But steam rollers are absolutely no good at dashing.

The Professor flew past on his bicycle in hot pursuit, but

the machine scattered a box of coloured marbles on the road and he side-slipped into the Mayor's arms.

'Thirty-five maids a dancing, ninety ladies singing, no end of a lot of swans splashing about, five golden rings,' sang the machine. It tore down Uppington Street, round the Square, turned left into Wright Street, hotly pursued by the Professor, his guests and crowds of Pagwell people who were shouting, 'Stop thief!' which was all they could think of to shout.

The machine ran out of presents and started picking up anything it could see and wrapping it in anything handy. A policeman held up his hand to make it stop and was given a piece of paving stone wrapped in an advertisement for second-hand bicycles.

On rushed the machine, across the High Street, smack into a smash-and-grab robber who was just dashing out of a jewellers shop with a sack full of valuables.

'And a partridge up a gum tree,' shouted the machine. It sat on the robber, tore open the sack and was only just stopped from handing out watches and pearl necklaces all round by the arrival of an absolute heap of policemen. They arrested the robber and would have arrested the machine too, only Professor Branestawm arrived just in time to turn off the works and explain what had happened, which the policemen didn't believe anyway.

'Disturbing the peace, y'know,' said a police sergeant with three chins. 'Conduct likely to cause . . .'

But the Professor and the Colonel between them had got the Christmas tree apart, packed it into a passing wheelbarrow, given a new fifty pence piece to the man who was pushing it and persuaded him to take it back to the Professor's house.

And everything turned out nicely because the jeweller

gave the Professor a reward for catching the robber, so the Professor was able to buy some very handsome presents to give to everyone at Christmas, which he did by the very unoriginal but completely satisfactory method of handing them over and saying, 'Happy um – ah – Christmas.'

12

The Peculiar Triumph of Professor Branestawm

'Excuse me, sir,' said the policeman.

'Yes?' said Professor Branestawm. He was driving along Broad Street in Pagwell, which was a very narrow street, in his own specially invented motor car that looked like almost anything except a motor car and made a noise like a bad tempered gramophone record played with a blunt needle.

The Professor thought perhaps the policeman wanted to know the time, but didn't think so very much because the clock on the Town Hall was going bong, boing, brang, boom, to say it was a quarter past something.

'You're going the wrong way, sir,' said the policeman.

'Er, ah, no, constable,' said the Professor. 'I am going the right way. I am going to Great Pagwell Library and this is the way to it, is it not?'

'Well yes sir, in a way,' said the policeman, scratching his ear. 'But this is a one way street, sir.'

'What of it?' asked the Professor, fiddling with levers that made the noise rather faster but no better. 'I'm only going one way along it.'

'Yes sir, but you're going the wrong way as I said, sir,' said the policeman, wishing it was his day off.

'You said this was the right way to Pagwell Library,' said the Professor. 'That must mean that this street leads to Pagwell Library, so how can I be going the wrong way along it? If I were going the other way I should be going away from Pagwell Library.'

'Yes, sir, that's quite correct, sir,' said the policeman, hopelessly, 'but you can only go along this street the opposite way to the way you are going.'

'Ridiculous!' said the Professor. 'Are you telling me that this is a one way street and the only way one can go along it is the wrong way?'

'Yes!' screeched the policeman, taking off his helmet and nearly jumping on it but remembering in time he would have to pay for a new one if he did.

'These traffic rules are absurd,' mumbled the Professor. He turned right round in his seat and began driving back the way he had come, which was easy because his specially invented car could go either way without turning around. It was an idea the Professor had got from the Pagwell trams.

Then he lost himself three times and finally arrived at Great Pagwell Library by a longer route than anyone had ever done before. He parked his car in a nice handy space that was strictly reserved for the Mayor, went into the library and asked for a book they didn't know they had.

'It must be in the store,' said one of the library ladies. 'If you'll just sit down, I'll get it for you.'

Now Great Pagwell Library was so full of books they had had to board a lot of them out, so to speak, in various buildings the Pagwell Council had bought for the purpose. The book the Professor wanted happened to be in a once-was sweet shop, four streets and three turnings away from the library, with traffic lights occurring as often as possible and always red when you wanted to cross. So it took the library lady a bit of a time to get there. Then she had to find the book, which meant ignoring enticing notices like 'Chummy's Chocs are Yummy' and 'Try our king size miniature mixture', and going up a staircase that was more like a bookcase.

But at last she found it and worked her way back through

red, amber and green traffic lights to the Professor. And he took a bit of finding, too, because instead of sitting down he had gone wandering round the library looking at the books and was finally tracked down in Sports and Pastimes reading a book called *Famous People I Have Shot* which ought to have been in Biographies because it was by a photographer sort of gentleman who had taken snapshots of notable people and called it that for fun. The Professor also had a few books stuffed in his pockets, one of which was a book about romance by moonlight which Mrs Flittersnoop had asked the Professor to get, only he got one about the night life of tabby-cats, which wasn't really what Mrs Flittersnoop meant.

By the time the library people had got things sorted out and politely squeezed the Professor out of the library it was ten minutes past closing time. By then the Professor had forgotten he had come in his specially invented motor car, and went happily home by bus, leaving his car most drastically disallowably parked in the Mayor's own private parking place.

'Mrs Flittersnoop!' cried the Professor next morning dashing into the kitchen and treading in the cat's breakfast. 'Fetch the police, my car has been stolen. Thieves! Ruffians! Miscreants! Dishonest persons! Help!'

Mrs Flittersnoop came creaking hurriedly down the stairs, but the Professor had dashed out of the house, smack into Colonel Dedshott who had arrived in answer to an invitation from the Professor. 'Come to dinner on Wednesday,' said the invitation, 'at 8 a.m.' Of course the Professor had meant 8 p.m. but he typed it, which he wasn't very good at, and had hit the wrong letter by mistake. Colonel Dedshott, of course, was one of those very 'Don't ask questions but obey orders' kind of soldiers and anyway he reckoned Professor Branestawm was quite likely to have dinner at breakfast time, so there he was. And there also were the Professor and Mrs Flittersnoop, both on their frantic way to the police station and the three of them got there in a sort of clump, with a lot of arm waving and talking sort of explanations.

'My, his, the Professor's car has been stolen!' cried all three of them at once.

'And the garage still locked,' cried the Professor looking through several pairs of glasses at once and seeing more policemen than the police station had in stock. 'Most mysterious.'

'Sounds like one of those sealed room mysteries,' said the police sergeant, who was rather a one for reading complicated whodunits. 'Any fingerprints?'

Just then Colonel Dedshott happened to look out of the window and saw the Professor's car in the police station yard, where it had been carefully brought the night before, from the Mayor's parking place.

'By Jove, Branestawm!' he cried. 'There's your car, right here at the police station.'

'What's that?' cried the Professor. 'My car here? Stolen by the police, disgraceful!'

'Fetch the Lord Chief Justice!' roared the Colonel. 'Serious matter this. Must be dealt with at top level, what! Outrageous, by Jove. Police stealing a man's car.'

'Oh dearie, dearie!' wailed Mrs Flittersnoop. 'It must be all these young fellows they're getting in the police these days. They're not like my sister Aggie's brother now, what's been in the force these twenty-five years, and never got into trouble, no and never been promoted neither, indeed sir.'

Colonel Dedshott made a grab at the telephone but the sergeant snatched it up first and the Colonel accidentally pressed a button which set off all the alarm bells in the police station. Instantly the room was crowded with two policemen, one of whom was the one who had tried to tell the Professor he was going the wrong way along a one way street. As soon as he saw the Professor he shot out again, knocking over a cup of tea which the other policeman was bringing in for the sergeant.

At last they got things sorted out, but not before Colonel Dedshott had nearly sent for the Chief Constable, most of Scotland Yard and General Shatterfortz. Then the Professor, the Colonel and Mrs Flittersnoop all went back to the Professor's house in his motor car, without losing the way more than once as it was only just round the corner.

'Something must be done about it,' said the Pagwell Councillor in charge of traffic.

'Something has got to be done about it,' said the Chief Library Man.

'Something will have to be done about it,' said the Mayor.

It was a highly special meeting of the Pagwell Council, and, of course, to find a way of dealing with Professor Branestawm, because not even five Pagwell Councils could have done that, but to find a way of dealing with two awkward problems that were sort of gumming up the works in Pagwell.

The Traffic Man was worried because too many people were parking their cars in streets and up lanes and in front of doors and on the paths and under bridges and making everywhere extremely difficult to get past.

The Library Man was all steamed up because there wasn't enough room for all the books and keeping lots of them in odd

buildings all over the place was definitely awkward for everyone concerned.

The Mayor was severely indignant about people leaving their cars in his own special official parking place. 'I know Professor Branestawm's the only one who's done it,' he said, 'but this sort of thing can spread and before we know where we are I shall have nowhere to park the mayoral car and have to come into town on a bicycle, and a nice thing that will be for Great Pagwell, the Mayor on a bicycle indeed!'

Everyone agreed, except a Councillor who kept a bicycle shop. But although they all agreed that something must be done, nobody could think what.

'Perhaps Professor Branestawm could invent a way or ways out of our difficulties?' suggested the Town Clerk.

Professor Branestawm's first idea was to charge everybody the most enormous sum of money to park a car anywhere, so that nobody would do it. But that would have meant everybody would want to come in by bus. And the buses were already full and a half and if they had more buses, they would take up even more room than cars, being that much bigger.

'And what about the books?' said the Library Man.

The Professor's next devastating thought was to have all cars fitted with special slopes, going up over the roof and down at the other end. 'It will then be possible,' explained the Professor, 'for several cars to be parked on top of one another and so reduce the amount of, um ah, space taken up.'

'What happens if the owner of the bottom or middle car of a pile wants to take his car away before those on top have gone?' asked the Town Clerk.

'And what about the books?' put in the Library Man.

That squashed that idea. The Professor had several others, including one for painting every car in Pagwell red, blue, green, brown or yellow and making a rule that only red cars could come into town on Monday, blue ones on Tuesday and so on. But as most people had to come in every day to work in banks and baker's shops and at solicitors and supermarkets and so on, crash went that idea.

'And what about the books?' wailed the Library Man very faintly.

At last Professor Branestawm, after a very heavy supper and being woken up twice by a thunderstorm and once by Mrs Flittersnoop's cat pulling down a trayful of jam jars while trying to climb up on a cupboard to get at next Sunday's joint, hit on a very dizzy-maker of an out-of-this-world idea for solving the car parking problem and the book store problem, both at once.

'My idea is simple in the extreme,' he explained to the Pagwell Councillors. And extreme it certainly was, though none too simple. It consisted of digging up the gardens outside Pagwell Library, building an enormous carpark underneath, plus an enormous store for books and then putting the gardens back again.

The only objection came from the Parks and Gardens Councillor who didn't see why his nice gardens should be dug up, and he didn't see how they could be put back again without disturbing the flowers, which didn't care much about being disturbed, being rather old-fashioned flowers and a bit set in their ways.

'I will invent special excavating machines,' said the Professor, 'so that the, ah, underground carpark can be dug out from under the gardens without disturbing them. I shall also arrange,' he went on, clashing his five pairs of spectacles about like anything, 'for the library to have special motor scooters with which to collect books from the more, ah, remote parts of the underground store.'

'The library staff will have to pass driving tests,' said the Traffic Councillor, who loved making people go in for tests and if possible failing them because they couldn't back a car into a space half an inch too small for it, first go, without touching the sides.

The great Branestawm Mechanical Underground Parking Garage and Automated Book Store was well on the way to not being finished in time. Ingenious digging machines were hard at it shovelling earth from under the library gardens while other machines carefully propped up the ground so that the gardens shouldn't fall in on top of everything.

Severe notices sprouted up all over the place, saying 'No admittance' and 'Keep out' and 'Nobody allowed in here unless wearing a metal hat.' This was just in case a bit of the gardens should, after all, fall on someone's head.

Industrious shouts of 'Clear that gangway a bit to the left, Jim!' and 'Don't make that there slope too steep now, Alf!' rang out in the Pagwell air. 'Puff puff puff, whizzy clanketty pop bang!' went Professor Branestawm's digging machines, and 'I'm digging for a wide carpark,' cried one of the workmen, adding, 'Jeeps may safely graze.' He sang in the church choir on Sundays and was a bit given to being a rare funny one on weekdays.

Earth, bricks, stones, long lost rubbish and municipal muck of all kinds were cheerfully dug up and flung accurately into new places. And a lot of people spent their lunch hours watching all this scientific activity, which was cheap enough as entertainment as it didn't cost anything, but was definitely unsatisfying as far as lunch went, which was nowhere at all, as there wasn't any.

The Traffic Councillor had a beautiful time not allowing anyone to park anywhere at any time for a week or two, while the streets were crammed with enormous trucks carrying the earth from under the gardens out into the country where it made a spectacular new hill.

The Drains Councillor was hopping about all over the place in a pretty panic in case some of his favourite drains got dug up in the excitement. But fortunately the only one that got in the way was a little skinny drain for carrying away the dregs and tea leaves from the Library Man's afternoon tea, and that was easily diverted without annoying anyone or emptying itself into the drain that carried away the Mayor's hand-washing water from the Town Hall.

There was a slight hitch one wizzy Wednesday when one of the machines dumped a shovelful of earth into a hole another machine was digging. The other machine dumped it back and there looked like being a bit of a mechanical fight, in which the other machines would probably have joined. But the whistle for lunch went off just in time and everything and everybody stopped instantly. Then after lunch the machines were in a better temper.

There were, of course, little things such as the Vicar being startled out of a new sermon he was thinking about while walking through the gardens, when a tree suddenly disappeared in front of him through a machine having dug up too much earth from under it. 'Dear me,' murmured the Vicar. 'This is most disturbing. I do hope this is not the work of the one below.' Which of course it actually was, though not quite in the way the Vicar meant.

At last the incredible project was finished.

'I fancy that without boasting,' said the Professor, 'this is a car-park and book store unlike anything else in the country or indeed in the, um, ah, world.'

It certainly was, or let's hope so.

To put a car in the park you simply drove it to the entrance and got out. But you had to be quick, because mechanical hands instantly took hold of the car, put it in a lift, and shot a little pink cardboard ticket at you. And if you weren't out of the car it put you in the lift too, which was against the rules and you were apt to be fined. 'If they can find you,' said the Traffic Man and thought it was an intensely funny joke.

Then your car went whizzy whizzy clank rumble, down down into the lowermost lowers where it was slid into place rather like a book being put on a shelf. And the pink ticket had numbers and things on it to tell the machine where to find the car when you wanted to take it out again.

All the cars were carefully parked under classes, just like the books in the library. Sports cars, whose owners were always telling tall stories about how fast they could go, went under Fiction. Elderly cars went under Historical, little teeny mini cars were to be found in a space marked Juvenile and so on.

There were special rules, of course, sort of borrowed from the Library, which didn't mind lending its rules as it was used to lending its books. But where in the Library if you kept a book out too long, they charged you a fine, in the car park they fined you if you left a car in too long.

There was even a car washing machine which washed, polished, disinfected, cleaned out, dusted and dolled up a car if you pushed the right button on the machine, which was quite easy as there was only one button on the machine. There were other highly clever machines that would fill the car with petrol, and water, both in the right places every time, mend punctures, see to brakes and generally boss a car about to see that it behaved itself.

Underneath the Library end was the book store, where the volume of volumes that could be kept was simply enormous.

And the Library girls had no end of a time chugging about getting books and sending them up to the Library. They became so expert at it that it became quicker to get a book from the store by the motor scooter girls than to find one yourself on the shelves upstairs. But there was a bit of reckless driving sometimes. Once a very urgent scooter girl with a load of books on high speed machinery collided with another girl carrying books on slow speed gardening, and some rather startled borrowers who wanted to know how to grow roses round their doors, got books explaining how to pack fifty thousand tins of sardines in tomato sauce in three minutes . . . flat, of course.

The underground library air was full of cries of 'Biography of Sir Joshua Jelligeorge, three volumes. Chugg a chugg, pop poppety pop honk honk!' and 'Make way for the new Encyclopaedia of Cycling' and 'Don't over-take me at an intersection with Gibbon's Roman Empire on my hands' and 'Why didn't you sound your horn before cutting in front of Progress and Posterity with Delay is Dangerous and Other Stories?'

'My word, Branestawm!' cried Colonel Dedshott, who tried to park his horse in the mechanical car park but fortunately failed as the parking machines were a bit above dealing with anything as small as one horsepower, and the cleaning machines might have sent it back with chromium plated hooves. 'This is a wonderful triumph. Working perfectly, by gad! Nothing going wrong, can hardly believe it what!'

'I trust, Dedshott,' said the Professor, rather loftily, 'that I have had sufficient experience of mechanical, um, ah, mechanics, to be able to avoid such unintentional, er, contre . . . that is to say accidental . . . er, there is no reason why my machine should go wrong,' he finished.

And oh, unbelievable, incredible, and not at all expected or understandable thing; nothing did go wrong with the machines. Cars of all kinds, sizes and prices were expertly parked in the right places without so much as a scratch on a hub cap, and brought out again and restored safely to their apprehensive owners. True, somebody took the Mayor's car out by mistake and brought it back full of ridiculous vegetables. But you couldn't blame the Professor's machines for that.

Professor Branestawm's name was all over the Pagwells. The newspapers published photos of him, right way up, standing outside the entrance to his car park. One photographer asked him to stand a little further back for one picture and the car parking machine scooped him up. Then, not being sure whether to park him under Science, or Curiosities, or Natural Phenomena, handed him over to the wash and polish machine. This shampooed his trousers, passed him to the other machines that filled his pockets with spare sparking plugs, cleaned his boots with petrol, adjusted his spectacles in the wrong order and sent him back to the surface with a bill for goodness knows how many pounds and frightful quantities of new pence.

Miss Frenzie of the Pagwell Publishing Company wrote a book about him with highly coloured pictures of the car park and even more highly coloured compliments.

'Well indeed I'm sure sir,' said Mrs Flittersnoop as she brought him his tea, with a special celebrating sort of iced cake made to look like a motor car standing on a library book that a friend of hers at the Pagwell Superbakery had made specially, in his spare time. 'I'm ever so glad you've had such a success that I am sir, not but what you deserve it.'

Everything was wonderful.

That night the amazing and incredibly successful underground car park and book store sprang a leak. Unreasonable quantities of Pagwell Canal got into the place without paying.

'Oh dear, oh dear!' cried the Professor, dashing round in his second best pyjamas and a hat. 'I might have known something would go wrong. But it isn't my machines this time. Nobody can blame me.'

Nobody in fact could blame anybody. That was the frightful thing about the whole affair. Extra heavy rain in the night had filled Pagwell Canal above its usual dirty water mark. Some geological fault in the ground had caused something to give way. Cracks occurred in the car park wall, and the canal came rushing in to see what was going on.

Fortunately there were no cars in the car park as it was night time. But the car parking machines were a bit messed up. And some of the water had got into the library store but only made a few of the books damp, and they were very dry books anyway.

Soon the book store wall was repaired and made canal-proof. But the car park was flooded and nothing could be done about that.

But ha! Couldn't something be done about it? It certainly could, and Professor Branestawm did it. He converted the flooded car park into an underground yacht basin where people could moor their boats instead of parking their cars. The machines were converted to nautical purposes. Car washing and polishing gave place to deck scrubbing and brass polishing. Anchors were mechanically sand-papered, things were made fast fore and aft, scuppers were un-scuppered and no end of bilge was efficiently dealt with.

And Professor Branestawm went down in world history as the first man to invent underground yachting.

But if you ever want to park a car in Pagwell, you'll find the simplest way to do it is to fit it with a rudder, some sails and an anchor, and float it down the Pagwell canal into Professor Branestawm's Library Underground Yacht Basin. And let's hope nobody pulls the plug out.

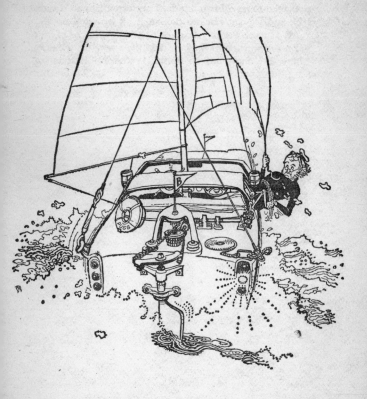

About the Author

Norman Hunter writes: 'I was not invented by Professor Branestawm. I was born. In London, 1899, a few years after the other Normans got there. After escaping from school I had a course in all-in wrestling with typewriters and eventually inserted myself into the advertising profession. I wrote advertisements of such allure that people bought vast quantities of the most unlikely things before they could stop themselves. I am also a conjurer and managed to let off two hundred performances at Maskelyne and Devant's before the Plazis hit it with a bomb.'

Mr Hunter was in Johannesburg for twenty years, but has now returned to England and lives near the Thames where he continues to write Professor Branestawm adventures.

Fattypuffs and Thinifers

ANDRE MAUROIS

Edmund Double loved food and was plump, like his
mother, while Terry his brother could hardly wait to
leave the table and was consequently very thin, like his
father. None the less, they were all very fond of each other
and the boys were amazed when, happening by chance
to take a moving staircase to the Country Under the
Earth, they found themselves split up and thrust head-
long into the midst of the dispute between the warring
nations of the Fattypuffs and the Thinifers.

The sparkle and easy humour of André Maurois' book
is certain to fascinate children of all ages as long as
Fattypuffs and Thinifers co-exist and remain mutually
indispensable.

The Kingdom of Carbonel

BARBARA SLEIGH

Carbonel King of the Cats needed help, to guard his two
royal kittens while he was away from his kingdom, and
so of course he turned to his old companions John and
Rosemary.

Of course they were proud to be entrusted with the
kittens – but it was a difficult job with such high-spirited
youngsters and especially with Queen Grisana of Broom-
hurst aided by Mrs Cantrip ever on the watch to trap
the kittens and invade Fallowhithe – but they hardly
expected it to lead to adventures like John's becoming
invisible or being run away with by a very dim-witted
magic rocking chair, and stranded all night on top of the
tallest building in Fallowhithe.

If you have read Barbara Sleigh's other Puffin book,
Carbonel, you will already know how much excitement
and entertainment she packs into her stories.

The Fox-Busters

DICK KING-SMITH

The Foxearth Fowls found their names on the bits of
writing scattered about the farm, like Fisons and Leyland,
Trespassers and Beware Of. And one day a bold rooster
bearing the noble old name of Massey-Harris became the
father of three chicks so exceptional that they were given
the honour of three brand new names, for it turned out
that the sisters Ransome, Sims and Jefferies could fly
faster, higher and further than any before them. And
when a group of determined young foxes, hungry for the
taste of chicken, kept laying plans for one fiendishly
cunning raid after another, the legendary three and their
mother found a way of outwitting the most crafty of them.
Not for nothing would they one day be known as the Fox
Busters!

Dragon in Danger

ROSEMARY MANNING

It was nearly the end of Sue's second holiday in Cornwall,
where her good friend R. Dragon had lived ever since
the days of King Arthur.

The green dragon was very sad to think Sue was going
so soon. She was the first human friend he had had for
hundreds of years, and he was going to miss her. Then he
had an idea – he would visit Sue in *her* home in St Aubyns.

But Sue was worried about it. How would he get
there? And where could he live? Not in her little house,
for sure. Well, one way and another R. Dragon got over
those difficulties, and he was soon nicely settled on an
island in St Aubyns, and was even invited to take the
star part in the local pageant. But wicked Mr Bogg and
Mr Snarkins began to plot against him.

For readers of seven and over.

Heard about the Puffin Club?

... it's a way of finding out more about Puffin books and authors, of winning prizes (in competitions), sharing jokes, a secret code, and perhaps seeing your name in print! When you join you get a copy of our magazine, *Puffin Post*, sent to you four times a year, a badge and a membership book.

For details of subscription and an application form, send a stamped addressed envelope to:

The Puffin Club Dept A
Penguin Books Limited
Bath Road
Harmondsworth
Middlesex UB7 ODA

and if you live in Australia, please write to:

The Australian Puffin Club
Penguin Books Australia Limited
P.O. Box 257
Ringwood
Victoria 3134